DJINN IN LOVE

MYSTICAL MATCHMAKERS

BOOK FOUR

C.C. WOOD

CHAPTER ONE

THIS WASN'T WORKING.

Jasper Bayat sighed as he walked his date out of the restaurant, his hand resting lightly on her lower back.

This was his third date in a week. Gillian was a lovely woman. Intelligent. Articulate. Cultured.

On paper, she was exactly what he said he wanted in a woman. Exactly what he said he wanted when he signed up for Mystical Matchmakers.

In reality...she bored him. Not only that, but she seemed to tense up any time he raised his voice above a murmur. Or frowned, even if it wasn't at her.

Based on her demeanor, their date wasn't what she expected either.

When they stopped next to her white Mercedes, Gillian squared her shoulders and faced him, obviously gearing up to let him down easy.

Jasper was tempted to beat her to the punch because he didn't want to waste any more time listening to her try to find the words to let him know that she didn't want to see him again.

1

C.C. WOOD

To his utter surprise, Gillian said, "You're a smart, handsome man, Jasper, but I don't think we need to bother with a second date."

He blinked at her. All night, she'd been so careful in choosing her words when she spoke that her sudden bluntness was a bit of a shock.

Once the surprise faded, he smiled. "You didn't seem to be enjoying yourself all that much. I'm sorry I wasn't better company."

Gillian cocked her head, studying him. "I think you would have been excellent company if you weren't distracted by whatever it is you were thinking about all night."

His smile faded. "I wasn't distracted."

It was Gillian's turn to grin up at him. "I've dated enough to know when a man has one hundred percent of his focus on me, Jasper. It was clear that you didn't. And that's okay. As I said, you're very smart, so I enjoyed our conversation, but I think we can both agree that we lack chemistry."

He fought the urge to scowl and shoved his hands in his pockets. Dammit, the woman was right. He had been distracted. And they did lack chemistry. He noticed that she was beautiful, but he wasn't attracted to her.

Finally, he relaxed and chuckled. "As I said, I'm sorry I wasn't better company. At least the food was delicious."

Gillian's smile grew. "That it was. Thank you for dinner." She reached out and squeezed his hand. "And good luck finding your match."

With that, she climbed into her Mercedes and drove away.

Jasper walked over to his SUV, folding his long frame into the driver's seat. As he started the car, his mind wandered to the subject that had been distracting him tonight.

Veronica Salt.

In the five weeks he'd been a member of Mystical Matchmakers, he'd spoken to her at least twice a week, sometimes more. Each time, it only cemented in his mind what he'd thought the day he met her.

She should have been his match. Not his matchmaker.

Two months ago, his mother insisted that he have a date for his brother's wedding. She offered to set him up with the daughter of a friend, which he turned down immediately and with vigor. For some insane reason, his mother thought that he needed a woman like her in his life. Someone outspoken, bossy, and independent.

While he admired all those qualities in his mother, he didn't want them in his romantic partner. Mostly because he was outspoken, bossy, and independent, so dating a woman just like him would only lead to arguments and him pulling out all his hair.

No, he needed someone who calmed the constant chaos in his head and cooled the fire of his temper. A woman who could stand up for herself, but whose strength was quiet rather than bold.

Until he'd walked into Mystical Matchmakers, Jasper had never met a woman like that. Not until he shook Veronica's hand.

Instantly, the eternal ticking of his thoughts slowed and his always simmering internal fire calmed. The inside of his head fell silent. He realized the feeling was true peace.

Every time he talked to her, the same thing happened.

But when he'd asked her if she ever dated the clients, she shook her head and said that clients were off-limits. Especially clients that she was working with personally.

For the next few weeks, he'd tried to move on and find another woman to take to his brother's wedding, but every date became less and less appealing. Especially when he spoke to Veronica after each one to give her feedback.

Now, he had a little more than a week until his brother's wedding and no date. He could already hear his mother introducing him to every single woman at the reception and pushing him to dance with all of them.

Shuddering, he put his car in drive and left the restaurant parking lot. He couldn't endure that. Not for the four-day event that would be his brother's wedding party.

No, he needed a date.

And it had to be Veronica Salt.

As he pondered the dilemma during his drive home, an idea popped into his head. One that should have alarm bells blaring in his mind, because the concept was unhinged.

But there was one thing he excelled at, in business and in life, and that was getting what he wanted.

He knew how to work hard. He wasn't afraid to take risks either.

This plan would require both of those things to be effective, including a huge risk of this blowing up in his face.

But, if he succeeded, the reward would be the woman he'd wanted since the first moment he saw her.

Oh, yes. Jasper was going to go through with his plan.

Because she was worth it.

Monday, he implemented the first step.

He left work an hour early and headed to the offices of Mystical Matchmakers. He would go in and tell Veronica that he no longer wanted his membership because the only woman he wanted to date was her. Then, he would find a way to convince her to give him a shot.

He glanced through the front windows as he approached the office and stopped. There was a man standing in front of Veronica's desk. He was smiling as he spoke to her. Then, the man winked at her and a pretty pink blush spread across her cheeks.

The fire that constantly burned in his belly, the fire of the djinn, flared. He fought his body's urge to expand with magic, wrestling with the instinct to turn the man into a toad. Or a braying jackass.

Jasper marched away from the window, his plan razed to ash. Instead, his fire ruled him.

He pulled the door open just as the man was exiting. The guy nodded at him, and he managed to return it. Barely.

When he walked through the door, the first thing he saw was her. The sun coming through the window highlighted the hints of purple in her hair even though it was pulled back into a long braid that draped over one shoulder.

All he could look at was her. He headed straight toward her desk, stopping just in front of it.

He hated the way her spine stiffened up when she saw him. It made the fury in him swell, even as it made his chest tight. He didn't want to cause her tension.

"Mr. Bayat."

"We need to talk."

He heard how loud his voice was, but there was nothing he could do it about it. He was barely hanging on to his control.

A tall blonde woman moved into his line of sight and held out her hand. "Of course we can chat. I'm Dominique Proxa, the owner of Mystical Matchmakers. I'm sorry we haven't met before."

He looked down at her hand, tempted to ignore it. Only knowing that Veronica would disapprove of the behavior had him wrapping his fingers around hers and giving it a short shake.

"Hello. I'm Jasper Bayat. It's nice to meet you, Ms. Proxa, but I would prefer to speak to Veronica."

He noticed that she was looking at Veronica and did the same. Veronica's posture was still ramrod straight and her face seemed pale. He didn't like that she seemed afraid. Of him.

He fought to tamp down his roiling emotions. To regain control.

She didn't know him well enough to understand that his anger wasn't directed at her. And he wasn't very good at hiding his emotions because he never bothered before. He had no doubt that she could see what he was feeling.

Dammit, why was he always off balance with this woman?

"You seem upset. Perhaps it's best if you tell me what's troubling you," Dominique said, drawing his attention away from Veronica.

A flash of annoyance spiked his temper again, but he ground his molars together and took a deep breath.

"I would prefer to deal with Veronica. She has been my point of contact since I started with your agency."

Good. His voice sounded calmer. More even.

Dominique opened her mouth, probably to argue with him, but Veronica interrupted. "Of course, Mr. Bayat. We can talk in the conference room. It's this way."

Jasper followed her as she rose from her chair and walked toward a small room to the right. The wall between the front part of the office and the room was glass, but they wouldn't be overheard inside.

When Veronica shut the door behind them, Jasper turned to face her.

"How was your date this weekend?" she asked.

He couldn't control his frown. "Gillian was a nice woman, but we weren't a good fit. That's why I'm here today."

Veronica tilted her head, nodding and listening without interrupting, so Jasper continued.

"I told you when I signed up that I needed a date for my brother's wedding. The event is this coming weekend. Even if Gillian was a good match for me, she likely wouldn't want to attend a four-day family event with me, even though we would have separate rooms."

He realized that the space between them was much larger than he wanted, so he moved around the table until he could see her face clearly.

"I don't have enough time to keep up with this trial and error. I need to confirm whoever my date will be this week. My brother is breathing down my neck about this because the wedding planner needs my date's name for the place cards at the reception. My mother is foaming at the mouth because I won't tell her anything about who I'm bringing and insisting on introducing me to a slew of "suitable" woman, none of whom I'm actually interested in dating. This process isn't working for me."

Veronica nodded. "You're right. Your date probably wouldn't be comfortable spending four days with you, even if you met her and hit it off today. But waiting until six weeks before your brother's wedding to start looking for a date might not have been the best choice."

She was right. But godsdammit, he was a busy male. And he hadn't realized his mother was going to insist he have a date or provide one for him, whether he agreed or not. Fuck. He had to get back to his plan.

"None of that matters. My sole purpose in coming here was to find a date for my brother's wedding. A woman I wouldn't mind spending time with. Someone I'd like to get to know better. You haven't fulfilled your end of the bargain…yet."

Veronica frowned at him. "What do you mean *yet?*"

"So far, you're the only woman I've met through Mystical Match-makers who I can tolerate. And, since you haven't found another woman to go with me, I think you should be my date."

There was a long silence as she stared at him in obvious disbelief.

"If this is a joke, it isn't funny," she stated, crossing her arms over her chest.

The hint of hurt in her expression made him clumsier than he already was. Jasper found himself fumbling his words. Something that very rarely happened to him. Most people accused him of being too blunt, but there was something about Veronica that left him nearly tongue-tied.

"It's not a joke and it definitely isn't funny," he said. "You owe me a date and, since you didn't manage to find a suitable match for me, you'll have to do the job."

"Do the job?"

"Either that or I cancel my membership and demand a full refund."

"We don't offer refunds unless you've been with our service for at least three months," she replied. "It was in the contract you signed."

"Then, I'm sure there are a lot of your current and potential clients that would like to know your service isn't effective or worth the cost."

Oh, holy shit, this conversation was going off the rails and in no way resembled what he intended to say to her. How had this happened? Then, he remembered the man who'd smiled and winked at her and found himself grinding his teeth again. That was right, he saw a man flirting with a woman he wanted to make his own.

He watched as Veronica closed her eyes and lowered her head, her shoulders slumping in defeat. Shit, shit, shit. This wasn't what he wanted. He tried to find the right words, a way out of this mess, but before he could come up with something that wasn't completely asinine, Veronica was speaking.

"We'll talk to Dominique. She could take over your file. Her magic makes her especially suited to finding your perfect match. I'll also suggest she offer you a refund since you did tell me that this was an important weekend for you and your family, and it was vital that you have a date."

"That's fine. But you'll also tell her that I asked you to go as my date."

"Fine."

Without looking at him again, Veronica headed toward the door. He followed without thought and their bodies crashed together just before they reached the door, her small frame colliding with his chest and abdomen. Her hands clutched at his waist for a moment before she jerked them away.

He heard her inhale sharply and saw the pink flush rush to her cheeks. She was blushing because she touched him. Surely that was a good sign.

Jasper grasped the door handle and opened it, allowing her to go first.

Her boss, Dominique, was sitting at Veronica's desk, clearly watching them through the glass wall. She got to her feet, her glimmering blue eyes meeting his. If he wasn't mistaken, she looked as though she was planning something.

Veronica spoke as soon as they reached her. "Dominique, I'm afraid Mr. Bayat is extremely upset with the matches he has been getting. I think perhaps you should take over his file and maybe even offer him a refund."

The blonde's brows rose as though she were surprised by her employee's words.

Jasper crossed his arms over his chest. It was time to regain control of this conversation and get back on track with his plan.

"I don't want a refund. I need a date to my brother's wedding this weekend. That was why I signed up for this service in the first place."

Dominique nodded. "I'm very sorry to hear that. Would you like me to see if I can arrange for you to meet someone in the next couple of days? Maybe she would be a suitable candidate."

The sentence wasn't complete before Jasper was shaking his head. "No, Veronica will attend with me."

He ignored the way Veronica stiffened next to him. His words weren't exactly what they'd agreed to, but she didn't say that. No, she remained silent.

As he watched Dominique, he saw her mouth tighten. If he wasn't mistaken, the blonde woman was trying not to smile. Hm, maybe she was an ally after all.

"Only if Veronica agrees," the woman stated, her tone firm.

Veronica's head snapped up, her body going rigid. "What?" she asked, her voice cracking as it rose higher in pitch.

Jasper ignored her. This was it. He was on his way to getting what he wanted. He'd find a way to fix the mess he'd made, and he'd do it fast. "She has."

"I'm glad that's settled then," Dominique said. "Once the wedding is over, please give me a chance to help you find the right match."

There was no way in hell that was happening. The only match he wanted was standing next to him, her body vibrating with surprise and confusion.

Satisfied that this encounter was back on track, Jasper smirked at the blonde woman. "We'll see."

When she smiled back, he wondered if it was because she was onto his machinations or she thought she'd gotten her way.

CHAPTER TWO

VERONICA COULDN'T FIND her bearings.

How had her conversation with Mr. Bayat devolved from getting him a date or a refund into her attending his brother's wedding with him? And *why in the hell* had her boss accepted the concept without blinking?

On autopilot, she gave Jasper her cell number when he asked for it. Veronica wasn't sure how it happened. She'd honestly thought he was joking when he said she would be his date. A joke in poor taste, but a joke, nonetheless.

So, when he said that she agreed to go with him, her mind had gone blank. Then, when Dominique had replied as though it was fine if she agreed, Veronica began to wonder if somewhere between the conference room and her desk, she'd somehow entered an alternate dimension.

After saying that he would be in touch with her later that evening, Jasper left the office, a smile on his face and a spring in his step. His satisfaction was so thick that she could almost see it wafting like a fog in his wake.

Of course, he would be smug and satisfied. He got what he wanted. A date for his brother's wedding.

But Veronica had no idea how she was going to get through it.

One, because Jasper Bayat was insanely attractive. Insane because she had difficulty keeping her thoughts from scattering when she saw him.

Two, he broadcasted his emotions openly. It was as if he didn't give a damn if people knew what he was feeling. As an empath, it was difficult to withstand. Her only saving grace was that the more time he spent with her, the calmer he seemed to be.

Third, he was a *client*. Though Dominique had no formal rules about dating clients, Veronica knew that it wasn't a good idea. So what if she'd made a comment to Dominique about helping her find some matches because she was so lonely?

That didn't mean she should be dating clients willy-nilly. Especially if those clients were tall, dark, and handsome djinns that made her heart race every time they looked at her.

By the gods, she wasn't going to be able to do this.

"You don't have to do it if you don't want to, you know," Dominique said, distracting Veronica from her careening thoughts.

"What?"

Dominique gestured toward the door that had just closed behind Jasper. "You don't have to go to this wedding. I'll give him a refund."

Veronica froze. Jasper had purchased their largest package, upfront, and it was worth over a thousand dollars. And her boss was willing to reimburse him in full.

No. She couldn't do that. Dominique had given her a chance when no one else would have. Half-fae, half-human empaths were not welcome in most supernatural circles.

To be honest, empaths of any ancestry were unwelcome. The only supernatural more reviled were telepaths because they could read minds rather than just emotions.

The new direction of her thoughts gave her an idea.

"No, don't give him a refund," Veronica said. "When he calls me tonight, I'll explain that I'm an empath. I doubt he'll want to take me when he finds out. Most males wouldn't."

Dominique frowned. "Don't talk about yourself like that," she said. "Any male would be lucky to have you as a date."

Veronica shot her a look because that had not been her experience.

Her boss shook her head. "Don't look at me like that either. The fact that people are intimidated by your ability to sense emotions is ridiculous to me. Most supernaturals have enough magic to shield if they want to. And you're not intrusive, nor do you violate boundaries when they've been set. Your abilities make you an asset in this business rather than a detriment."

"Thank you, Dominique," Veronica said. "I don't tell you often enough how much I appreciate the opportunities you've given me—"

The taller woman waved her words away. "You don't need to thank me. You were more than qualified for this job. Let's get back to the handsome Mr. Bayat."

Veronica bit back a sigh. "Do we have to?"

Her boss ignored her. "Are you not attracted to him?"

"I'd have to be dead to not be attracted to him," Veronica murmured.

Laughing, Dominique asked, "Do you not enjoy his company?"

Honestly, Veronica enjoyed talking to him even though his emotions were always loud and sometimes abrasive. He never hid his thoughts or feelings. He was honest in his actions and words. To the point of bluntness.

Veronica appreciated that. Whatever he said to her, his intense emotions always backed up his words.

Subterfuge was always the most difficult thing for her to deal with as an empath because the conflict between a person's words and emotions gave her a splitting headache.

"I do like talking to him. He's funny in a sneaky, biting way."

Dominique shrugged. "Then, what's the problem?"

"Well, he doesn't know I'm an empath for one."

"And?" Dominique asked.

"You don't think that will be enough to make him run away?"

Her boss shook her head. "Any other male, maybe. Jasper Bayat, I doubt it. That man is a bulldozer in a suit. Plus, I'm asking you how *you* feel about possibly dating him. Not how you think he'll feel about you. You can't control any of that, so it's best for you to focus on what you want out of a potential relationship."

"Okay," Veronica countered. "Then, I don't want to date a man who's going out with me because I'm the only one available. I want a man who wants me for me, not someone desperate for a warm body to prop up beside him at a wedding."

Dominique arched her brows. "Oh, so that's why he didn't take his eyes off you when he came in? Because he's so desperate for a warm body to prop up beside him?"

"He was upset when he came in. I'm sure even you felt that."

"Oh, yes, he was upset, but I don't think it was because he didn't have a date for the wedding. I think it was because the only woman he wants to take to said wedding was laughing and blushing with another man while he watched from the front window."

Veronica gaped at her. "What on earth are you talking about?"

"You blushed when Torin winked at you. I didn't realize it was Jasper at the time, but I saw someone standing at the front window, looking in. Now that I'm looking back at the situation, I'm almost positive that was him. And that the sight of you flirting with another man upset him more than his lack of date for his brother's wedding."

A short bark of laughter escaped Veronica. "I wasn't flirting with Torin! He's living with someone. I was just happy for him!"

"I know, but he's also extremely hot. Even my temperature rose a couple of degrees when he winked at you, and I have no romantic interest in him in the least."

Veronica's mouth open and closed several times. She had no idea how to respond to that.

"All I'm saying is that I think Jasper Bayat likes you. And that he wanted you to be his date rather than just viewing you as a faceless woman to drag around what's surely to be a stressful family event." With a smile, Dominique patted her arm. "Just try to be open to the idea that Jasper likes you. You might be surprised."

With that, her boss disappeared into her office.

Veronica went back to her desk and sat down, but she had no idea what to do next.

LESS THAN AN HOUR LATER, VERONICA GOT A TEXT FROM Jasper, asking her to meet him for dinner at an Italian restaurant not far from her office.

Her first instinct was to say no, but she decided it was best to rip the band-aid off and tell him tonight that she was an empath. Plus, she really liked the restaurant he named, and she rarely went there because it was a little expensive and didn't fit well into her budget.

Delicious pasta and limoncello cake would ease the sting of rejection after she explained what she was, so she would make an exception tonight.

After staring at the text for five minutes, Veronica finally texted him back.

> Veronica: I'll be there at six.

Jasper didn't make her wait for his reply.

> Jasper: I'll be waiting.

Oh, how those words made her feel. To know that a man like Jasper would be waiting for her. To know that when she left work that night, she had somewhere to go and someone who wanted to see her.

It was what she'd dreamed of since she realized that her abilities meant she would never have a normal life or a normal relationship.

A short time later, she walked into *Intermezzo*. The maître d' greeted her with a smile.

"I'm meeting a friend," Veronica said. "Jasper Bayat."

"Of course. Mr. Bayat has arranged a private room. Please follow me."

A private room? She didn't even realize *Intermezzo* had private rooms.

Veronica followed the maître d' around the side of the dining area to a hallway. He turned into the second door on his left, holding it open for her.

She nodded to him as she walked through and almost tripped over her own feet when she saw Jasper seated at a table set with lit candles and delicate stemware.

He looked like her every romantic fantasy come to life.

Not because he was beautiful, though he certainly was. No, it was because he'd obviously gone to some effort for tonight. Reserving a private room. Candles. A bottle of white wine chilling in a bucket beside the table. The way he stood when she entered the room.

The maître d' left them alone, but Veronica didn't even notice.

Jasper stood next to the table, unmoving. She realized with a jolt that he was waiting for her to sit down before he did. Someone in his life had taught him old-fashioned manners.

Veronica moved to the table, hooking her bag over the back of the other chair. "Hi."

"Hi, Veronica," he replied.

She swallowed when he said her name. His voice was warm. So were his eyes. And his emotions were calm. Much calmer than they had been when he came into the office earlier.

He moved around the table to pull out her chair. "I thought this would be best. It will give us a chance to talk and get to know each other."

"Okay," she agreed.

He scooted her chair beneath the table when she sat down and picked up the wine from the bucket.

"Do you like white wine?" he asked.

Veronica nodded, watching as he poured them each a glass. Once he tucked the bottle back into the ice bucket, Veronica took a sip. It was delicious. Light, crisp, slightly sweet.

"Do you like it?" he asked as he settled back into his chair.

"Yes. It's very good."

He smiled at her, which made him even more handsome. And approachable.

Veronica took another sip of wine, this one much bigger. More of a gulp, really.

Then, he shocked her further by saying, "I had to answer so many questions about myself when I joined Mystical Matchmakers that I feel like you probably know me pretty well now. Especially since we've been talking every week. Tell me a little more about yourself."

"What do you want to know?" she asked, caught off guard.

She thought they would be getting together to discuss the logistics of going to his brother's wedding. Not talking to each other like this was a real...date.

But it wasn't a real date. He wanted them to appear as though they'd been dating for a little while, this was just setting up the foundation. Right?

"What do you do for fun?" he asked.

Veronica cleared her throat. Normally, she wouldn't talk as much about her hobbies on a first date since they were nothing exciting, but, since this wasn't technically a date, she decided to be one hundred percent honest.

"I like to read. And I like to cook."

"What's your favorite thing to cook?" he asked.

"Thai yellow curry."

Another smile tugged at his mouth. "Spicy. I like that."

A blush rushed into her cheeks.

"What's your favorite book?"

Veronica shrugged, feeling a little more comfortable with this subject. "I don't really have one. It's usually whatever I'm reading at the time."

"Okay, what are you reading right now?"

Her blush intensified until her face felt like it was about to melt from the heat.

"Now, I'm really intrigued," he said, picking up his wineglass.

Hoping to fortify herself, Veronica copied his movement, drinking her own wine.

"Ready to tell me now?" he asked when she lowered her glass.

She decided to continue to be completely honest. "It's a romance novel by an author I really like, Brynne Asher."

"What's it called?" he asked.

She studied him but could only feel sincerity and curiosity radiating from him. He wasn't judging her or humoring her. He genuinely wanted to know.

"It's called *Illicit*. I've been waiting for it to release for a while." She toyed with the stem of her wineglass. "What do you usually read?"

During his intake interview, he said he enjoyed reading books, but didn't go into detail.

Jasper shrugged. "I mostly read thrillers and horror. Sometimes, I'll pick up a biography or some other non-fiction title that's getting a lot of attention because I feel like I should try to enrich my mind."

Veronica smiled at his words. "I think reading enriches your mind, no matter the genre."

He tapped his wineglass against hers. "I like the way you think."

Her shoulders relaxed at his words.

A woman came in carrying a charcuterie board. She smiled at both of them as she set it in the center of the table. "Is there anything else I can bring you at the moment?"

Jasper looked at Veronica, waiting for her to speak. When she shook her head, he answered, "No, thank you."

She moved to a table by the door and brought back two menus. "I'll return shortly to take your order for dinner."

Still smiling, she left the room.

Veronica knew she was in over her head. He wanted her to convince his family they were dating, and she was ready to believe they were, too. They weren't even halfway through this date. Meeting. Whatever this was.

"Tell me more about your family," she said, picking up a piece of cheese from the board. "If you want them to believe we're actually dating, I probably need to know something about them."

He seemed surprised by her words. "If I want them to believe we're actually dating?" he repeated.

She forced herself to pop the cheese into her mouth and chew as she nodded.

He leaned back in his chair, crossing his arms over his chest. "I thought this was a date."

Veronica blinked at him, feeling utterly pinned by those dark brown eyes. And the sensation of...hurt that seemed to be coming from him. It wasn't intense, but it was there.

Before she could grasp onto the emotion, Jasper began speaking.

"My brother is two years younger than me. And since he met Prema and they started dating, it was clear he was serious about her. My mother's been on my back ever since to find a nice woman and settle down. In her mind, as the oldest, I should be the first one to get married. The fact that I haven't is driving her nuts, so she's determined to take me along for the ride on the insanity bus."

Veronica laughed at his words and the dry delivery.

"Do your parents give you a hard time about being single?" he asked.

Her humor vanished immediately. His question reminded her of her plan. The plan to get him to drop this fake dating nonsense. But now, she didn't want to say it. Not when the evening had been lovely so far and he'd gone to so much trouble.

"Did I say something wrong?" he asked.

Veronica shook her head. "No, no. You didn't." She drained the rest of her wine, setting the empty glass back on the table. "My parents don't expect me to form relationships or eventually get married. They know it will be very difficult for me to find a man who could accept me."

He scowled at her. "Why in the hell would they think that? You're perfect."

Though he looked angry, Veronica could sense that it wasn't directed toward her, but rather her parents. And his words...they made her entire body feel warm. He thought she was perfect? If he did, he was the only one.

Her face flushed again, something she hated. Her fair skin meant that she blushed easily.

"I'm an empath. I sense the emotions of others and, sometimes, their thoughts come through as well. I can't read your mind, but, if you project your thoughts with enough strength, I can hear them."

She fidgeted with her empty wineglass, looking down at her fingers as she explained. She didn't want to see the change in his expression as she continued to speak.

"Almost every man I've dated has ghosted me when I tell him that I'm an empath. The few that didn't eventually broke up with me because they felt like they didn't have true privacy."

Veronica left out the part about how exhausted she was by the end of the day, and how difficult it was to block out her partner's emotions because she needed to rest and relax her mental shields. How she couldn't protect herself from her boyfriends' negative emotions, whether they were directed toward her or not.

Jasper's mouth pressed into a firm line as he listened, the tiny muscles in his jaw flickering when he clenched his teeth together. She squirmed in her seat, waiting for the onslaught of anger to burst out of him now that he knew the truth.

Once again, he surprised her. He was angry, definitely, but once again, it wasn't directed toward her. The emotion shimmered around him, but somehow never touched her. It was just…there.

"You can't help who you are," he stated, his voice rumbling from his chest. "And it sounds like you try to block out as much as you can around others because you want to protect their privacy."

He paused when she nodded before continuing, "And it makes me wonder why a man would need that kind of privacy unless he had things to hide."

Veronica shook her head at his words. "No, no. I understood. No one wants their partner to be privy to every little thought or burst of emotions they're dealing with. To feel like they're being spied on in their own home."

She shrugged at the deeper scowl that crossed his face. "Everyone has bad days, Jasper. Or bad thoughts from time to time. The knowledge that the person you're closest to can see or feel all that can be intimidating. Especially if you know she's too exhausted at the end of the day to block you out."

It was Jasper's turn to shake his head. "No, Veronica. Anyone who is honest about what they're thinking and feeling wouldn't be intimidated by a woman who can sense them. They would work on their own mental shields so they could give her a break when she got home. They would talk to her about what they're feeling or thinking, share it with her, rather than bombarding her with it all and pretending it wasn't happening."

Before she could argue or say any of the things she'd said before, the server came back, her wide smile still firmly planted across her face.

Without looking at the menu, Veronica ordered her favorite orzo with shrimp and asparagus. The light, lemony sauce that accompanied it would pair well with the white wine that Jasper had selected.

Jasper ordered chicken under a brick and nodded when the woman offered to top off their wineglasses.

As soon as they were alone again, Veronica said, "Sharing thoughts and feelings is a choice. Some people don't like it when that choice is no longer offered to them. I can't blame them. I wouldn't like it either if the shoe was on the other foot."

Jasper leaned forward. "Then, they shouldn't date an empath. If you were as honest with your past boyfriends as you've been with me, they knew what they were getting into and decided to date you anyway. It seems to me like they used your abilities as a shitty excuse when things weren't working out rather than talking to you about it like adults."

Veronica rubbed her forehead. This conversation was moving in circles.

As though he were the empath, Jasper changed the subject.

Through the rest of their meal, he told her more about his brother, his parents, and his soon-to-be-sister-in-law, Prema.

He also asked her more questions about herself, like where she went to college, if she liked to watch television or movies, and her favorite restaurants. The conversation remained light and easy.

And his emotions seemed dampened, as though he were actively trying to control them. That alone made Veronica feel lightheaded. Before he knew what she could do, his emotions had swirled around him, charging the very air. Now, it was clear that he was aware of his ability to broadcast and that he was actively trying to hold his emotions in check.

He even insisted on getting dessert, asking her to order her favorite. In turn, she insisted that they share it because there was no way she could eat it all by herself. The limoncello cake was three layers and the kitchen always sent out huge slices.

They were still chatting about the wedding the following weekend when Veronica glanced at her watch and saw that it was nearly nine p.m.

When he saw her face, Jasper asked, "What's wrong?"

"It's nearly nine," she said. "I need to get home soon. I have some things to take care of first thing in the morning before work."

Though she tried to argue, Jasper insisted on paying the bill. His hand rested lightly on her lower back as they walked through the nearly empty restaurant and out the door. His fingertips were hot enough that she felt them through the fabric of her silk blouse.

He was a djinn. She remembered that from his intake interview. Some were associated with water. Others with fire. There were others that utilized the elements of earth and air, but they tended to be friendlier and less aggressive than water or fire djinn.

Considering the heat emanating from his hand and his body, Veronica assumed his element was fire. Which would explain why he smelled a little smoky. The undertone of smoke accented whatever cologne he wore, making her imagine curling up in front of a fireplace with him.

No, she couldn't think like that.

She stopped next to her car, reaching for the door handle, too lost in her thoughts to notice the way Jasper watched her. He nudged her to one side and opened the door. The car unlocked automatically since she carried her key fob in her purse.

"Let me know when you've made it home safely," he murmured. "And we'll talk tomorrow."

Veronica blinked, breaking out of her thoughts, and looked up at him. "I will."

He leaned forward and she froze, unable to process what was happening. The scent of smoke, sandalwood, and amber assailed her as his lips brushed her cheek. His skin was so much warmer than hers that it almost felt as though she were standing in front of a fire.

"Goodnight, Veronica," he whispered next to her ear.

She couldn't help it. She shivered as the words seemed to vibrate on her skin.

Somehow, she managed to get into her car, start it, and pull away without embarrassing herself or hitting any stationary objects. She glanced in the rearview mirror as she drove and saw that Jasper was watching her.

Veronica tore her eyes away from him. Tonight was probably the best first date she'd ever been on. No, the best date all together.

She gave herself a mental shake. No. No. It wasn't a date. She couldn't afford to let herself believe this was real. He only needed a date for his brother's wedding. That was it.

She was a means to an end for him. She couldn't let herself forget that. Otherwise, she would end up hurt.

CHAPTER THREE

AFTER LAST NIGHT, Jasper was beginning to understand Veronica a little better. She was still a mystery to him in so many ways, but he'd learned something important during their dinner.

Not because of the words she spoke or the way she answered his questions.

It was the way she braced for his reaction when she shared that she was an empath. She expected him to withdraw from her. Maybe even tell her that he changed his mind, and he didn't want her to come with him to the wedding that weekend.

She was so used to being rejected that she automatically expected it.

It had enraged him. She was a beautiful woman. She was kind and gentle and everything that a man could want. Not a man. Him. Everything that he wanted.

He also hadn't missed how she shivered when he'd kissed her cheek and wished her a goodnight. She had her defenses up with him, but she was affected. Even if she didn't want to be.

That was why the first thing he did after he got to the office was order flowers. He remembered what she said yesterday about becoming easily overwhelmed and made sure to choose a bouquet that didn't have any blooms with a strong scent. He also asked that the flowers be in pastel colors.

He was just finishing the order when his brother walked into his office without knocking. Jasper shot him an exasperated look and turned his back while he talked to the florist.

When he was done, he disconnected to face Milo.

"What are you doing here, little brother?" he asked. "Aren't you supposed to have the week off to prepare for the wedding?"

His brother slouched in one of the chairs facing his desk, his legs sprawled out in front of him. "Mom called me at six a.m. this morning and insisted I come in to finish some paperwork." He chuckled. "I really think she just wanted to get in a few last-minute instructions before the wedding festivities begin on Thursday."

Jasper had to grin. That sounded just like his mother. He'd inherited his control freak tendencies from her. In fact, his mother made him look adjusted. As far as Leila Bayat was concerned, no one else could do things without her input.

Jasper had learned a long time ago to laugh about it rather than let it bother him. It was laugh or let her drive him insane.

"She also asked me again if I knew who you were bringing to the wedding," Milo said, smirking at him.

Jasper rubbed his forehead with two fingers. "You didn't tell her anything, did you?"

Milo tilted his head back to rest on the chair. "No, but only because I don't know anything." His smirk turned into a huge smile. "I'm beginning to think you've made this woman up just to get Mom to leave you alone. Though, I think you're old enough by now to know how that will backfire on you."

Jasper scowled at his younger brother. "I didn't make her up. She just required...convincing."

Milo's grin became absolutely toothy. Jasper wondered if that's what smaller fish saw right before the great white shark chewed them up. His brother might seem more mellow than the rest of the family, but he had the same killer instinct they all shared. Only he dressed it up with a friendly smile and twinkling black eyes.

"I'm guessing the flowers you spent the last ten minutes ordering are for her," Milo said.

Jasper didn't answer, mostly because his brother didn't give him a chance. Though it was clear Milo had been eavesdropping outside the door before he came inside.

"I'm also wondering why you didn't just have Margot send a bouquet for you. She has excellent taste, and she usually handles this sort of thing, right?"

Margot, Jasper's assistant, had been with the company since his father started it. She was a siren and, even at the ripe old age of four hundred and three, she looked no more than forty. She did have excellent taste. And she also ordered flowers for the women Jasper dated.

But Veronica was different.

His brother sat up straight in his chair, his smile fading. He looked shocked. "Oh, wow. You really like this one, don't you?"

"She is ..." Jasper wasn't sure how to describe her to his brother. He had too many words rather than too few. "She's exactly who I've been looking for."

"And you're bringing her to my wedding? Are you nuts?!" his brother exclaimed, jumping to his feet to pace in front of Jasper's desk, waving his hands as he spoke. "Her first introduction to Mom and Dad will be while we're surrounded by our crazy family. Auntie Samira is coming, and she's bringing Cousin Mina. Dad's entire family will be here, and you know how they are! They're going to have the two of you betrothed and making appointments to look at wedding venues before the rehearsal dinner is even over!"

Jasper shrugged. He didn't really have a problem with any of that.

His brother's eyes opened wide. "You don't just like her. She's the one!"

"Lower your voice before Mom ends up in here," Jasper hissed, leaning over his desk.

Milo mirrored his position until their faces were only a foot apart. "I'm right though, aren't I? She's the one. That's why you ordered the flowers yourself. And why you're bringing her to the wedding. Wait." He paused. "Didn't you say earlier that she needed *convincing*?"

Knowing where this was going, Jasper sat down in his chair and leaned back. "Yes. She did."

His little brother threw his head back and laughed, making Jasper wish they weren't in the office so he could sucker punch him in the gut. Unfortunately, his mother had forbidden that type of behavior as soon as they started to work at the family business.

Not that it stopped them completely, but they did try to keep any… *friendly* violence out of the office. Their mother had a point when she said their employees wouldn't respect them if they acted like children.

"Why did she need convincing?" Milo asked, grinning at him from across the desk. "And how did you manage it without scaring her off?"

Jasper shrugged. "She works at the matchmaking office."

"Matchmaking office? *You* went to a matchmaker?!" Milo chortled with glee. "Does mother know?"

Glowering, Jasper shook his head and came around from behind his desk. He went to office door, peeking out to make sure his mother wasn't lurking nearby. She didn't exactly spy on her sons, but she wouldn't hesitate to eavesdrop if she overheard them having a discussion that sounded interesting.

Satisfied that his mother wasn't going to overhear, Jasper shut and locked his office door before he turned back to his younger brother.

"No, Mom doesn't know," Jasper answered, "because if she did, she wouldn't be speaking to me right now."

"I think she'd be pleased," Milo retorted, settling back into the chair behind Jasper's desk.

The little shit had parked his ass on it as soon as Jasper turned his back.

Ignoring the obvious bait for his reaction, Jasper settled a hip on the front edge of his desk, his side turned toward his brother.

"No, she wouldn't. She'd be pissed because she's a control freak, and she thinks she knows best when it comes to who we should be dating. Hell, she practically handpicked Prema for you!"

Milo nodded. "That's true, but she was right. Prema was perfect for me."

"She is, but Mom always understood you a lot better than she understood me."

"That's because you're just like her," Milo retorted, which made Jasper roll his eyes. His brother smirked as he continued speaking, "You're a control freak, too. That's why you can't trust her to find you a woman. And why your first reaction when she tries is resistance, even if the woman is perfect for you."

Jasper scoffed. "None of the women she picks out are perfect for me because they're all just like her."

"And?"

"And you're right. I'm more like Mom than I am Dad. I don't need to marry someone just like me. We'd kill each other within months. I need someone more like Dad. Someone who calms my fire, not matches it."

His brother made a face as he considered Jasper's words.

"What?" Jasper asked in exasperation when the silence went on too long.

Milo grinned as he pushed himself to his feet. "Oh, nothing. I'm just enjoying the fact that you admitted I was right about something." He pretended to buff his fingernails on his chest. "It's the best wedding present you could've given me."

"Fuck you," Jasper replied, but it was without heat.

Milo came around the desk and clapped a hand on his older brother's shoulder. "You're also right that you need someone who calms your fire instead of feeding it. A woman like Mom or you would go head-to-head with you on everything. Considering how tightly wound you are here at work, that's the last thing you need at home."

"Double fuck you." Despite his words, Jasper laughed.

"I'll back you up with Mom this weekend," Milo assured him. "And I can't wait to meet the girl who required convincing. You're almost as pretty as me, so I find that shocking."

Jasper couldn't let that insult go. His fist shot out and connected with Milo's ribs. His little brother grunted, hunching forward at the contact.

"One, she's a woman, not a girl. And two, I'm not pretty, I'm handsome."

"It was a compliment," Milo rasped.

"Sure, it was," Jasper said.

"What's her name anyway?"

"Veronica. Veronica Salt."

"Like the chick from the movie about the chocolate factory?" Milo asked.

"No, that's *Veruca Salt*. And don't bring that up because I'm sure she gets it all the time," Jasper insisted.

Milo raised his hands in surrender. "No worries, big bro. I'm sure Mom will go there before any of us ever could anyway."

Jasper let his head fall forward and pinched the bridge of his nose. By the fire in his veins, his brother was on a roll today with his observations. Because he was right again. Leila Bayat would be the first to make a snarky comment about Veronica's name.

Shit. Maybe he should have pursued Veronica well before now so he could have introduced her to his mother in a calmer setting. A setting that he had complete control over so he could whisk Veronica away if it was clear that his overbearing mother would be too much for her.

Milo patted his shoulder again, this time in sincere sympathy. "I mean it, Jasper. I'll have your back with Mom at the wedding. And Aunt Samira. And the others." When Jasper lifted his head, his younger brother squeezed his shoulder. "Besides, as soon as they realize how much you like her, they'll go straight from making sure she's good enough for their precious baby boy to trying to mold her into the perfect Bayat bride."

Jasper had no words as his brother sauntered to the door and unlocked it.

"See you Thursday night at the resort," Milo said, waving a hand before he left the room.

Jasper stared at the empty doorway for several minutes, trying to figure out the best way to move forward. It was already Tuesday. There wasn't enough time to arrange a casual drink or meal with his parents and Veronica before they left for the resort Wednesday morning. Milo, his fiancée, and their parents would be at the resort the day before the weekend festivities began on Thursday. What began as a small family wedding had become a gigantic extravaganza with every person Milo and Prema or their parents knew getting an invitation.

His only option was to make sure that Veronica was as comfortable as possible with him before they left. If she trusted him, she would lean on him when she needed it. Or tell him when she needed a break.

He pulled his phone out of his pocket. He needed to see her again. Today.

CHAPTER FOUR

VERONICA TRIED to ignore her phone when it dinged, but she couldn't. Not when there was so much going on at the office today and Dominique was out for meetings with clients until after lunch. Her boss needed to hire someone else and soon. They were so swamped with work that they could barely keep up.

With a sigh, she made sure to save the progress she'd been making on the spreadsheet before she picked up her phone from the desk. A message from Jasper waited for her.

> Jasper: I want to see you tonight. Are you free?

Veronica couldn't stop the smile that tugged at her mouth. She enjoyed her dinner with Jasper last night and, once she got home and was no longer overwhelmed by his presence, she realized that he had enjoyed it as well. Even though he'd tried to erect a mental shield, a few of his emotions had leaked through. At the time, she'd been too nervous to truly let it sink in, but in the dark peace of her bedroom she finally took the time to process what she'd felt from him.

Still, she didn't want to get her hopes up. Jasper made it clear that he was only interested in a date for his brother's wedding. And past experience told her that very few men could handle her abilities over a longer period of time.

As she stared at his question, disappointment overwhelmed the fragile hope. Though she wanted to see him tonight, there was no way she could manage it. She had a late intake interview scheduled at six and that wouldn't be done until at least seven, maybe seven-thirty if the client needed a little more handholding.

With a sigh, Veronica replied to his text.

> Veronica: I would love to, but I have to work late.

Three dots immediately appeared at the bottom of the text string, as though he'd been waiting by the phone for her reply. Nerves shimmered in her belly. God, this felt too real.

> Jasper: Lunch tomorrow? I have an appt close to your office in the early afternoon.

> I can do lunch. 1 p.m. work?

The three dots reappeared again, but Veronica was distracted by the door to the office opening. She frowned as she glanced at the clock. Her next appointment wasn't for a couple of hours.

But it wasn't a client. It was delivery. The woman smiled at her as she carried a beautiful flower arrangement up to her desk.

"Veronica Salt?" she asked.

"That's me."

The woman held out the flowers, but Veronica stared at them blankly until she spoke again, "These are for you, hon."

"Oh!" Veronica got to her feet and took the bouquet from the woman. "Wow. These are lovely."

"They are. The gentleman who ordered them put a lot of thought into'em," the woman agreed with a wink. She whipped a small tablet out of one pocket and a stylus out of the other. "If you'll just sign here."

Veronica set the vase on the corner of her desk and signed her name on the line the woman indicated, wondering what the woman meant about the thought behind the bouquet.

"Thank you," she murmured as the woman marched out of the office.

Veronica didn't look up as the door shut, leaving her alone again. That giddy feeling was back in her belly, only this time it was stronger. She noticed the card nestled between a tulip and dahlia. With gentle fingers, she plucked it free and opened it.

I enjoyed your company last night.
Looking forward to this weekend.
~ Jasper

The bubbly nerves in her belly burst and swelled into her chest. She fanned her suddenly warm face with the card. Jasper wasn't behaving as she expected. Based on his words yesterday, she assumed that they would meet once or twice to get their story straight before the wedding and he would treat her more as an employee or acquaintance than a date.

But this was a gesture a man made when he liked a woman. No, when he was *courting* a woman.

Her phone chimed and vibrated against her desk, distracting her from her racing thoughts.

Veronica moved the flowers to the opposite corner of her desk so she could see them even when she was working on her computer and sat down. She didn't take the time to read Jasper's text. She was too focused on figuring out how to word her thanks without seeming too...desperate? Emotional? She had no idea what to call the feeling swelling inside her, only that she'd never experienced it before.

Which was frightening in and of itself because Veronica thought she'd been through the entire spectrum of emotions, either through her own heart or vicariously through those around her.

After typing and deleting her message at least five times, Veronica settled on something appropriately gracious but hopefully not too effusive.

> Veronica: Thank you for the flowers. They are beautiful.

She didn't add that she was looking forward to the weekend too because it would have been a white lie. While she was looking forward to spending more time with Jasper, she wasn't happy about the mental chaos that accompanied events that drew large crowds. Especially if Jasper's family was anything like him.

If his relatives broadcast their emotions as intensely as Jasper, Veronica wasn't sure how she would make it through the four days of wedding festivities in one piece. Or with her sanity intact.

Once again, his reply was immediate.

> Jasper: You're welcome. I have a meeting, but we'll talk tonight and decide where to eat tomorrow.

> Veronica: Ok.

As she set her phone to the side, Veronica glanced at the flowers on her desk one more time. Their fragrance was light and delicate, and the pastel petals blended in a gentle rainbow.

She wondered again what the woman meant when she said that Jasper had put a lot of thought into them. Had he chosen exactly what flowers were in this bouquet? Or just the color scheme? Or was the woman just saying that because it sounded good?

Shaking her head, Veronica shoved that last thought out of her head. In her experiences with Jasper over the past few weeks, one thing had been very clear—he was honest to a fault. Even if it was to his own detriment.

There was no way he would have asked this woman to lie and make him look better. It wasn't in his nature and Veronica didn't need her empathic abilities to understand that. She only had to recall every interaction they'd had thus far.

With a quiet sigh, she pushed her circling thoughts about Jasper to the side. Right now, she had a great deal of work to do and very little time to accomplish it.

⁂

SEVERAL HOURS LATER, VERONICA WAS JUST FINISHING UP the intake interview with a new client. The woman in question was a siren named Selene. Her magic and the effect her voice had on any man nearby presented a few challenges, but Veronica was confident that they could work together to get past them. Maybe by starting off with text messages or emails. And then moving to phone calls.

A siren's magic wouldn't work as well on someone who cared about them. Or someone they cared about as well. By establishing a connection before she spoke to them over the phone or saw them in person, maybe they could mitigate any potential issues that might arise from Selene's power.

That was the sad fact about supernaturals like Selene. And Veronica. Their magic attracted people to them, but usually not for the right reasons. Men, and women, often wanted to abuse Veronica's power, using it for their own personal gain.

And Selene could never know if the men she spoke with in passing were truly attracted to her—her personality, her heart, and her mind. Or if they were drawn to her because of the pull of her voice and the beauty her magic had granted her.

Veronica walked Selene out of the conference room where she'd conducted the intake interview. Veronica was explaining the next steps in the intake process when the door to the office opened. They both looked up, startled by the sound.

A young man walked in with a white food container wrapped in a plastic bag in his hands. He grinned when he saw them and came deeper into the office. His eyes widened when he got a load of Selene, his gaze locked on her as he walked closer.

"Veronica Salt?" he asked Selene.

She took a step, shaking her head.

Somehow, the young man tore his gaze away from her and looked at Veronica. "You Veronica Salt?"

"Yes. How can I help you?"

He came close enough to hold out the container. "Delivery from Thai House for you."

Blinking, Veronica found herself automatically taking the plastic wrapped container. "But I didn't order anything."

The boy pulled the receipt off the bag. "Let's see. Name on the credit card is Jasper Bay...Bay..."

"Bayat?" Veronica asked.

"Yeah. Jasper Bayat. Know him?"

Veronica bit her lip and nodded. The guy was already heading back toward the door before she was able to speak again.

"Wait. Let me get you a tip!" she said.

Without turning around, he waved a hand. "Already taken care of."

When the door shut behind him, Selene asked, "Who's Jasper?"

Veronica carried the container to her desk and set it down. She wasn't sure how to answer the question. She couldn't say he was a client. That would sound unprofessional. She also couldn't say her boyfriend because they'd only been on one date.

Selene smiled down at her. She was a tall, willowy blonde who looked like a supermodel. She also wore high heels that meant she towered over Veronica. "Is he your boyfriend?"

Veronica managed to smile back. "Not really. We just started... uh...dating," she murmured.

"Well, he must like you a lot if he's sending you dinner."

Veronica's smile no longer felt forced. "He wanted to take me to dinner, but I couldn't meet him tonight."

"So, he sent you dinner instead," Selene continued.

Veronica answered with a nod.

Selene's smile grew wider. "Like I said, he must like you a lot." Her eyes moved to Veronica's desk, snagging on the flowers. "Did he send you those?"

Heat worked its way up from Veronica's neck to her cheeks. "Yes. Earlier this afternoon."

"Definitely likes you," Selene repeated.

Veronica put her hands over her cheeks. Her fingers felt cool against her burning face.

As though she sensed Veronica's discomfort, Selene changed the subject. "Speaking of dinner, I'm starving. I'm going to head out."

"Oh, you don't have to," Veronica started. "I'm sure you have questions or things you'd like to discuss."

"I literally can't think of any questions right now because my stomach is growling so loudly. You said you would be calling me next week with a game plan, so I'll write down any concerns I have, and we can address them then."

"Really, it's no trouble—"

Selene shook her head. "It's fine, Ms. Salt. It's nearly seven-thirty. We'll talk next week."

With that, Selene turned on an elegant heel and swayed to the door. Her strides were long and graceful, and her footsteps were nearly soundless.

As the door shut behind her, Veronica realized that Selene was exactly the kind of woman she would have paired with Jasper. The thought pierced her, sharp and cold, like a needle in her flesh. Her hands trembled as she moved around her desk to sit in her chair.

In her mind's eye, she could almost see the two of them together. In her heels, Selene would be nearly eye level with Jasper, her slender figure and gleaming blonde hair the perfect foil for his dark, intense good looks. The image was so clear and focused, like a photograph. It made her stomach ache. Especially when she thought about Jasper moving on after this weekend and asking for more matches.

The tremor in her hands moved to her arms and legs, causing the chair to creak. Dear God, if he wanted to continue on as a client, would he expect her to provide him with matches?

They weren't even truly dating, and it was already painful to think about setting him up with another woman.

Veronica took a deep breath. No, she couldn't think like this. They weren't dating. She couldn't let herself get attached to him. No matter what kind of generous gestures Jasper threw her way. She had to stay aloof, distant, in order to protect herself.

It had been so long since a man seemed to care about her. About whether she ate dinner. Or sending her flowers to share that he was thinking of her.

Well, the flowers hadn't happened before, but there had been times her previous boyfriend had texted her or called her just to talk because he said he missed her. That sort of behavior ended shortly after their relationship became more serious and he realized how much her empathic abilities affected her life.

It wasn't much longer before he broke things off with her.

Veronica had to stop thinking of Jasper as the man she was dating and remember that he was a client. Otherwise, she would get hurt.

Taking a deep breath, she closed her eyes. She held the air in her lungs until her chest grew tight and then released it in a slow, steady stream. Then, she repeated the process again. And again.

After the third breath, her emotions were much calmer. She picked up her phone and texted Jasper

> Veronica: Thank you for dinner. I enjoy this restaurant a lot. I didn't even know they delivered.

Unlike this morning, his reply wasn't immediate. She was already unwrapping the plastic bag from the food container when her phone chimed.

> Jasper: You're welcome. And you should look into this app called DoorDash. It's quite handy.

Veronica snorted as she chuckled. His dry, sarcastic sense of humor came through in his text message clearly. She could almost imagine the smirk on his face as he typed the words.

> Veronica: I'll keep that in mind for the next time I'm working late.

The three dots appeared beneath her message and then disappeared. Then, they reappeared. This happened several times before Jasper's text finally came through.

> Jasper: Enjoy your yellow curry. I'll call you around nine, if that's okay.

Veronica's first reaction was a resounding yes, but then she hesitated. They had only been talking for two days, yet she was already getting attached. What would happen after his brother's wedding was over and he expected her to find matches for him? Or worse, she never heard from him again?

Before she could work through her thoughts and figure out what to do, Jasper texted her again.

> Jasper: I emailed the itinerary to you and we need to go over the particulars for Milo's wedding.

Veronica sighed. No matter what happened after this weekend, she had already committed to being Jasper's date. She loathed breaking promises because she felt how much it affected those around her when other people did it.

> Veronica: 9 is fine. I'm going to eat and finish up some work so I can get home. Thanks again.

> Jasper: You're welcome. Text me before you leave and when you get home so I know you made it safely.

> Veronica: I will.

A knot formed in Veronica's chest, twisting and coiling, making it difficult to breathe. The number of people who cared about her safety was a precious few. Her parents. She counted Dominique, even though her boss had an aloof demeanor. Dominique demonstrated she cared in her own way and Veronica had even sensed her affection a few times, even though Dominique's mental shields were as solid as stone.

Veronica blinked rapidly, willing away the tears that formed in her eyes. She couldn't get used to this. To a man caring. She knew better.

He wouldn't stick around. Not after he realized how much work she was and that she exhausted him like she had with her past relationships.

She had to be honest with herself and keep her eyes wide open. It was the only way to protect herself from heartbreak.

CHAPTER FIVE

HE STUDIED the phone in his hand, wondering if he'd come on too strong today. Veronica's texts after her dinner had been delivered seemed...different. Earlier, her replies came quickly and seemed casual.

This evening, it took her much longer to answer. Her words seemed carefully chosen, almost terse. Like when she texted him to let him know she'd left the office and again when she made it home. Two words each time. He'd sent a message back each time, acknowledging that he got them, but she didn't respond to either.

> Veronica: Heading out.
>
> Veronica: Home safe.

His instincts were one of his greatest assets in business and they were telling him he'd fucked up somehow. He would ask her tomorrow when he saw her for lunch. He wanted to see her eyes and read her expression when she responded.

Jasper grunted and glanced at the time again. Eight-thirty.

He wished that he'd decided to deliver her dinner himself. Then, he could have spent the evening with her again. Even if it meant watching her work instead of talking to her. Instead, he'd decided to give her space, worried that he'd overwhelm her if he pushed his presence on her.

After their conversation last night about how tiring it was to keep her mental shields up all day and then for hours in the evening, Jasper was keenly aware of his own emotions and how they spilled out of him. He hadn't practiced his mental shields in a long time. Until he was sure that he could maintain them around Veronica, he wouldn't crowd her.

She'd been more concerned about how he might feel about an invasion of his private thoughts and feelings, but Jasper noticed the way her shoulders sagged when she discussed her past relationships and how much work it took to keep her mind protected when she should have been able to relax and just be herself.

He glanced at the clock again. Eight-fifty. Fuck it.

Jasper clicked on her name in his phone list and lifted the device to his ear.

"Hi, Jasper." Veronica's voice was soft. Hesitant.

"Hi, Veronica. How was your dinner?"

He could hear the smile in her voice when she answered. "It was delicious. Thank you again."

"Where do you want to eat tomorrow for lunch? I'll be close to your office. Is there another restaurant nearby that you like?"

"There's a French bistro a couple of blocks away."

"Do you eat there often?" he asked, intensely curious about her likes and dislikes.

From their conversation last night, Jasper sensed that Veronica was different from most of the women he knew. Not that there was anything wrong with the women he'd dated in the past. It was just... the way her mind worked struck him as different. Maybe it was because of her ability. Or maybe it was her personality. She seemed to see the world from a completely different perspective—one he very much wanted to understand.

"No, I usually bring my lunch to work," she answered after a brief hesitation.

Jasper wondered if it was because she wanted to save money or if it was less stressful to eat at her desk than to go to a crowded restaurant and try to eat with people around. He wouldn't ask though.

Instead, he said, "I was thinking I could pick something up for both of us and bring it to your office. We need to discuss details for the weekend since we're leaving Thursday afternoon for the resort."

She didn't say anything for a moment. Then, she asked, "I thought that was why we were speaking tonight."

Jasper chuckled. "Yes and no. I emailed you the dress suggestions my soon-to-be sister-in-law sent me and the itinerary for the weekend." He paused. "We'll need to leave Thursday afternoon around two. Will that be a problem?"

Her silence worried him, until she sighed. "No. Dominique has already given me Thursday and Friday off work."

She didn't sound happy about it.

Guilt crept into Jasper's gut. He was tempted to tell her not to worry about it, that he would attend alone, but instinct told him that he would never get another chance to win her over.

Instead, he asked, "What can I do to make this easier for you?"

"Make it easier for me?" Veronica repeated, her voice cracking the end of her question.

"Yes. What can I do to make sure that you aren't overwhelmed during the circus that has become my brother's wedding?"

She laughed a little. "Circus? Will there be monkeys?"

"Absolutely. But don't tell my little brother that we bought him from that family of chimps, okay?"

Veronica laughed again. This time the sound was freer and lighter. Jasper wanted to hear her laugh like that every single day. It was soft, much like her voice, but warm.

Her giggle died away and silence fell between them. He was just about to speak when she finally answered his question. "It helps if I can take short breaks during long events. If there's time for me to go back to the room between the wedding and the reception or a chance for me to get away from a crowd for five minutes, it keeps me from being exhausted before the night is over."

He could do that. He would find her a quiet place to relax every hour if he had to.

"I'm sorry."

He blinked at her apology. "What? Why?"

"I know you're probably regretting your decision to take me as your date."

"No, I'm not," he stated. He realized that his voice was harsher than he intended and found himself doing something he never did. He explained himself. "I'm not sorry that you're going to be my date. I would rather take you to the wedding than any of the women I've met in the past six weeks."

He heard her shaky exhale at his words before she replied, "Okay."

"Good. Now, let's talk about what you'll need to know about my family and the different events happening this weekend. I should warn you that everything in my family ends up being over-the-top, so between Thursday evening and the wedding Saturday evening, there are no less than four gatherings. You don't have to attend all of them, but I'll have to be there, so we'll need to figure out how to make it work."

"Okay," she repeated. Her answer was stronger this time.

ANTICIPATION BUZZED IN VERONICA'S VEINS. SHE shouldn't be nervous or excited about seeing Jasper. She shouldn't be feeling any of the things she was feeling. Nor should she believe what he'd said last night.

But she did. Oh, she did.

Her stomach had skittered when Jasper said he only wanted to take her to the wedding. Not any of the other women she'd matched him with over the past few weeks. The way his voice deepened. Just remembering it made shivers break out over her skin.

43

They had talked until after ten o'clock at night. It wasn't until she'd yawned a second time that he said he would see her at lunch.

Now, it was closing in on one o'clock and Jasper would be arriving any minute.

Nerves danced in her stomach and chest. This felt like more than a simple meeting to prepare for a weekend of being his fake wedding date. A lot more.

Veronica was trying to concentrate on the computer screen in front of her when the front door to the office opened. She jumped and looked up in time to see Jasper step inside, a large brown paper bag dangling from one hand and a drink carrier in his other.

When he saw her staring at him, he smiled. A smile that widened as he approached her desk, his black eyes sparkling and revealing a small dimple in one cheek. Veronica realized that she'd never seen that dimple before because his smile had never been quite so big.

"Good afternoon, Veronica," Jasper said, stopping in front of her desk. "How are you today?"

"Um, good," she answered, feeling her mouth hesitate to form the word.

The man was too good-looking. He made her want to stutter.

"Are you ready for lunch or do you need to finish something up?"

She swallowed hard and got to her feet. "I'm ready for lunch," she answered, wiping her hands down the sides of her skirt. Her palms were suddenly damp. "Thank you for bringing it."

Jasper shrugged. "No problem at all."

"I thought we could eat in the conference room," Veronica started to say.

Before she could finish, Dominique's door opened and her boss stepped out, leaning a shoulder against the doorjamb. "Mr. Bayat," she said, nodding to Jasper.

"Ms. Proxa."

A smile graced Dominique's mouth. "Please call me Dominique." Her eyes dropped to the bag and drinks in his hands. "Ah, you brought Veronica lunch. Excellent. We've been so busy this week that she hasn't been eating properly,"

Veronica felt her face heat and knew her cheeks were so bright that they probably glowed red. While her boss wasn't exaggerating, they had been swamped, Veronica hadn't been eating much due to her nerves about this weekend rather than being busy. But she wasn't about to admit that to Jasper.

Veronica shot her boss a wide-eyed glare, using her facial expression to encourage her to shut up. Dominique merely looked back at her and raised a single eyebrow.

"Well, Jasper and I have some things to talk about," Veronica said. "But I will listen for the phone so I can answer it."

Dominique scoffed. "You'll do no such thing. You'll have your lunch and relax. I'll handle the phones and, if for some reason I can't answer, they can leave a message on the machine. It won't hurt them if they can't get an immediate answer."

Veronica opened her mouth to argue, but Jasper gently nudged her with his hip. "No problem. Thanks, Dominique."

Her boss shot him a knowing look and a quick wink, which made Veronica flush further. When she glanced up at Jasper, he was studying her with amusement tinged with intensity. He watched her like he expected her to run and was preparing to chase her if necessary.

"Shall we?" he asked, gesturing toward the conference room with the hand holding their drinks.

Veronica nodded, pulling her bottom lip between her teeth. She walked in front of him and held the door open. His broad body herded her toward the far corner of the table and her heart rate kicked up when the door shut behind them.

Jasper set the bag and drink carrier on the table, taking everything out of the bag and setting it on the table before her.

Feeling awkward, Veronica smoothed her hands down the front of her skirt again. "Thank you for bringing me lunch."

Shoot, she'd already said that. Hadn't she? Her equilibrium was shot around him.

"I wanted to see you before tomorrow's chaos," he murmured. Once the paper bag was empty, he folded it up and set it to the side.

"Let's sit."

Again, nerves shimmered in her stomach when he pulled the chair out for her, his knuckles brushing her back when she sat down, and he pushed it in.

"Thanks," she all but whispered.

"Stop thanking me," he commanded, his voice deep and soft.

Veronica's cheeks heated again, and she knew her blush was rushing up to her hairline. Why was she reacting to him like this?

Scratch that. She knew. After everything he said last night, Veronica was beginning to believe that he might be interested in dating her even after his brother's wedding.

As they sat down and opened their containers, Jasper asked her, "Can you be ready to leave at eleven tomorrow morning? I thought we could stop for lunch on the way to the resort. That will give us enough time to get ready for the party at six."

"I can be ready," she answered, excitement fizzing in her belly at his words.

He wanted to take her out to lunch. If he wasn't interested in her, surely, he wouldn't want to take her out for a meal before they left the city. Right?

The wedding was at an exclusive resort two and a half, nearly three, hours out of the city and the first event scheduled was a party meant to welcome all the guests who were able to come two days early. There were more events on Friday, as well as the wedding and reception on Saturday. Each one had a different dress code. Jasper offered to take her shopping when they were on the phone last night, but Veronica assured him she didn't need to purchase anything for the events.

He'd argued for a bit, but she explained that her time working at Mystical Matchmakers had involved attending all kinds of events from cocktail parties to galas. While her wardrobe might be a bit boring, it would be adequate for the long weekend. It had taken her longer than she expected to convince Jasper, but he'd eventually relented and accepted her insistence that she didn't need new clothing.

"I asked my mother to arrange for us to have adjoining rooms," he continued. "I wanted to keep up the appearance that we've been dating but I also wanted you to be comfortable."

God, Jasper was so unexpected. He was so blunt and abrupt that she could barely believe how considerate he was being. Once again, he was trying to shield her from his emotions. She could tell by the muted sensations she experienced around him. It was clear he was out of practice because they occasionally leaked through.

Like right now. She could tell he was sincere. He wanted to have lunch with her the next day before they drove to the resort. He wanted her to be comfortable. He genuinely liked her.

Maybe it was time for her to be as honest about her feelings as Jasper was about his. She took a breath, preparing to ask him if what was happening between them was real. If he wanted to keep seeing her after the wedding.

But his phone rang, the opening strains of Run the World (Girls) filled the conference room. Grimacing, Jasper put down his plastic fork and fished his phone out of his pocket.

"Sorry. It's my mother. I have to answer it because, not only is she my mother, she's also my boss."

Veronica bit back a smile, both at his words and the ringtone. But she couldn't stop it from spreading across her face when she heard his next words.

Lifting the phone to his ear, Jasper said, "Hi, Mom. I see you've figured out my passcode yet again. Nice pick for the ringtone."

Veronica couldn't hear anything his mom said, but she shamelessly listened to Jasper's side of the conversation.

"Oh, I see. You bribed my little brother to do it. I thought you preferred to do your own dirty work."

Though his words were said in a stern tone, his mental shields had dropped a bit, and Veronica could sense his affection for his mother. And healthy doses of mild irritation and amusement. Resting her chin on her hand, Veronica turned her body so that she faced Jasper, and her elbow was propped on the table.

He noted the movement out of the corner of his eye and glanced over at her. He winked when he saw her smile, which made that fizzing sensation return to her belly.

"What was that?" he asked, breaking the trance she'd fallen into. "Mom, I'm not coming down until tomorrow. I told you that." He paused. "Her name is Veronica, remember? She has to work today and I'm sure she needs time to pack and handle her own stuff before she leaves for four days."

The fizzy sensation turned into lead bubbles that fell directly into the pit of her stomach. He'd talked to his mom about her. She reached for her drink, hoping to wash away the heaviness in her gut.

"She's very special. I have no doubt you'll love her and that Dad will ask me how I managed to convince someone so far out of my league to date me."

Veronica had just taken a sip from her straw when he said those words and immediately choked on the iced tea and lemonade mixture. Coughing uncontrollably, she shoved her chair back from the table. She didn't want to interrupt Jasper's conversation by choking to death.

Before she could get to her feet and walk out of the room to give him privacy, Jasper's hand clamped down on her knee, holding her in place. Veronica's body stiffened, but his fingers remained wrapped around her leg. The heat of his palm seared the bare skin of her thigh where her skirt had ridden up. Veronica stiffened but didn't try to pull away.

By the time she stopped coughing, Jasper was off the phone and had turned his chair to face her completely.

"Are you okay?" he asked.

She nodded, clearing her throat one last time before she answered, "I'm fine."

"I know I warned you once, but I should warn you again. My mother is a handful. She's great, but she will steamroll right over you if you let her." When he saw the look on her face, he chuckled. "Don't worry. I'll protect you this weekend. I'm just warning you in case she manages to get you alone."

Veronica nodded again. If Jasper's mother was anything like him, she was going to be difficult to say no to.

"I hate to cut our lunch short, but I have to get back to work." He released her knee and got to his feet. "But I'll see you tomorrow at eleven."

"I'll be ready," she replied.

He gathered his food and drink. Unlike Veronica, he'd already eaten most of his lunch. "If you need anything, don't hesitate to call or text me."

Jasper leaned over her chair and Veronica stared up at him from her seat, frozen by his sudden nearness. His lips pressed against her cheek, perilously close to the corner of her mouth. The breath stuttered in her lungs and her throat closed.

He pulled back a few inches, but his face was still so close to hers that she could see that his eyes weren't actually black, but a deep, dark brown. From this close, she could see the difference between his pupils and irises.

"You'll call or text if you need anything, right?" he repeated.

"I will," she murmured.

He smiled at her before he leaned closer and kissed her cheek again. This time his mouth brushed the edge of her lips. Veronica bit back a moan and locked her hands around the arms of her chair to control the full-body shudder that threatened to move through her.

"Bye, Veronica."

Oh, no. She had to speak. Her throat was so tight that she wasn't sure she could. She cleared her throat. "Thank you for lunch. It was delicious." Veronica pushed herself to her feet. "I'll walk you out."

"No, you stay and finish your food. I'll call you later if I get out of the office early enough. With my brother out of the office all week, I'm doing his work and mine, so I may not have time."

She started to argue, but he was already moving out the door of the conference room and heading to the front of the office. Veronica watched as he strode out of Mystical Matchmakers and let the door swing shut behind him.

She was more confused now than she had been earlier. And she hadn't been able to ask him about what was happening between them.

Maybe it was for the best. It had been so long since she'd truly been attracted to anyone that Veronica wasn't sure that she was seeing Jasper's behavior in the proper light.

She would pretend to be his girlfriend this weekend. If he seemed interested in more, she would ask after the wedding.

It would be better that way.

CHAPTER SIX

JASPER WAS LOOKING FORWARD to having Veronica all to himself this weekend.

Well, not completely to himself.

They would be around his family, but neither of them would have to work and there would be down time between all the parties, gatherings, and events. She would be with him constantly for four days.

Any other woman, and he would be preparing himself to have her constantly underfoot. He would be plotting ways to spend time alone. There were very few women he could tolerate for prolonged periods of time. But with Veronica...he wanted to be around her as much as possible.

She'd been quiet when he picked her up from her apartment, other than apologizing for having two suitcases. She laughed when he told her his mother would have twice that amount.

When they stopped for lunch, the smile on her face was bright and surprised. The restaurant he'd chosen was in a little cottage and the entire place was Alice in Wonderland-themed, from the décor to the menu. He would never have gone if she wasn't with him, but he would do it again and again if it put the sparkle of delight in her eyes and the wide smile on her face.

Some of her reserve dropped away. Veronica chatted with him, chuckling over the names of the cocktails and dishes on the menu. When he tried to order her a Rabbit Hole cocktail, her laughter and playful shove to his arm were the most unrestrained she'd ever been with him. Instead, she'd ordered a glass of the Queen of Hearts sangria, saying she couldn't resist when she saw sangria listed on any drink menu.

Jasper filed that piece of information away in his mind, just like he had when she told him that she liked Thai food and romance novels. He understood now why his father did things like that for his mother. And how much she seemed to appreciate them.

After lunch, she was a bit more relaxed, and they talked more the last hour of the drive. He warned her about his Aunt Samira. He explained that she had good intentions, but she was also determined to see all the children in the family married off now that most of them were grown. His cousin, Mina, was Samira's daughter and she always aided and abetted her mother in these endeavors because she didn't want her mother to start in on her.

He also gave her more details about Milo and his fiancée, Prema. He wanted her to feel comfortable and prepared when she met everyone. Based on his interactions with Veronica, Jasper sensed that she was Type A in terms of her personality. She wanted a plan when going into any situation, whether social or professional. He was doing his best to give her the information she would need to create one.

When they took the exit for the resort, Veronica began to fidget, twisting her fingers together as she stared out the window. Jasper reached over, resting his hand over hers.

"The only people at the hotel right now are my parents, Prema's parents and sister, and my brother. You won't have to deal with a big crowd just yet."

She threw him an apologetic look. "I'm sorry."

"Don't apologize," he commanded. Throwing a quick glance toward her, he said, "Just promise me you won't run away tonight."

A startled laugh burst out of her. "What? Why would I run away?"

He slowed the vehicle, turning next to the sign for Devil's Playground. "After you deal with my family this afternoon and evening, you'll be tempted."

Veronica shook her head. "If they're anything like you, they can't be that bad."

Jasper shrugged. "Okay, then, promise me that if you're going to leave, you'll take me with you. Because they are that bad. I'm just the best of them."

She giggled again, the sound filling his vehicle. He squeezed her hand with his before he released her and parked the car in front of the main lodge.

Jasper turned toward her just as she leaned over to kiss his cheek. Her lips landed on his and Veronica jolted with a squeak. Before she could pull away completely, he cupped her cheek in his hand, rubbing his thumb over her bottom lip.

When she took a shaky breath, his eyes lifted to hers. Then, he said what he'd been wanting to say since Monday.

"The only woman I've wanted to date since I joined Mystical Matchmakers is you."

Veronica blinked, staring back up at him in confusion. "What?"

"After you turned me down the third time I asked you on a date, I stopped because I didn't want to make you uncomfortable."

A furrow appeared between her brows. "Then, why did you basically blackmail me into coming to the wedding with you?"

Jasper shrugged. "I said I'm the best of my family, not that I'm a good guy. I'm not above exploiting a weakness when necessary if it gets me what I want."

A flush spread across her cheeks.

"A wedding with my entire crazy family wouldn't be my choice for a third date, but I'll take what I can get and ask for more."

"Ask for more?" she repeated.

His thumb skimmed across her lower lip again. "I want to kiss you. Will you let me?"

The pink on her cheeks deepened. Her eyes grew heavy, and her breathing became unsteady. He heard her swallow before she opened her mouth and answered, "Yes."

Though she agreed, Jasper took his time. He leaned forward, giving her a chance to change her mind. He kept his eyes locked on hers until their lips touched. Veronica inhaled, a small sound escaping her, before her eyes fluttered shut.

He traced the tip of his tongue over her lip, enjoying the softness of her flesh. Her mouth opened against his, her tongue slipping out to meet his. She tasted like the sangria she drank with lunch and the apple tartlet they'd shared for dessert.

Jasper curved his hand around the back of her neck, sliding his fingers into the hair at her nape. Her mouth opened wider against his and let him inside. Using his hold on her hair, he pulled her closer.

A breathy moan escaped her, vibrating against his tongue. Jasper tried to lean closer, to remove the distance between them. But his elbow hit the steering wheel, and the horn blared, echoing around them.

Veronica jolted, pulling away. Her eyelids were heavy, and her mouth was wet and swollen. She looked dazed and thoroughly kissed.

Jasper leaned forward, intent on kissing her again, when his brother's ugly face appeared on the other side of the passenger window as he rapped the glass with his knuckles. Veronica yelped, whirling around to see who was knocking on her window.

Biting back a string of foul language, Jasper unbuckled his seatbelt. "Don't move. I'll get rid of him and open your door."

He didn't wait for her to reply, just hauled his body out of the car and rounded the front end. Jasper didn't stop moving until his body bumped Milo's. His brother's cheeky grin didn't dim in the least as he backed up.

"What's up, big bro?" he asked. When he tried to lower his head to take another peek at Veronica, Jasper put his hand flat against his brother's chest. "Aw, c'mon. I just wanted to say hi."

Keeping his voice low, Jasper answered him, "Veronica is shy. Her family is small and not that close. She's not used to people like you or me. Or our family. I want her to be comfortable this weekend and not run away screaming, never to take my calls again. So, tone it the fuck down for now, okay?"

With each word that Jasper spoke, his brother's eyebrows rose higher and higher until he looked as though his eyes were about to pop out of his head. "Holy shit. You really do like her."

Jasper released a disgusted sigh. "I thought we already established this."

"Yeah, but I figured you'd be over the infatuation by today. It's obvious that you're in even deeper than before."

"And this surprises you, why?" Jasper asked. "I told you she was different. That she was the only woman I've wanted like this. Ever."

At his words, Milo took a step back. "Okay. Understood. I'll watch my step for now and help you keep Mom and Dad in line tonight. But you know she's going to see us as our true selves before the night is over. With Auntie Samira and Mina being here for the cocktail party and the rest of our cousins and friends coming in tomorrow, the typical Bayat family craziness will make an appearance sooner rather than later."

"I know, Milo. I just want to give her a chance to meet you, Prema, and Mom and Dad before I throw her in the deep end."

The passenger door to his car opened, nudging him in the hip. Jasper stepped back, taking hold of the door handle, and pulling it the rest of the way open. Veronica looked up at him, her cheeks still pink, but her eyes were sparking with irritation.

"If you need to talk to your brother, I can wait inside," she said.

Before Jasper could speak, his brother jumped right in. "My brother was just making sure I would be on my best behavior so you wouldn't realize that our entire family is completely nuts and order an Uber to escape as quickly as possible."

Jasper elbowed his little brother in the gut, making him grunt and take a step back. "He's partially right. I wanted to make sure he didn't act like the heathen he is right off the bat. Obviously, it's too late."

The annoyance vanished off Veronica's face as she watched them. A smile tugged at the corners of her mouth. "Okay, then I'd like to go inside."

Jasper reached out, took her hand, and helped her out of the car. Her long hair glinted in the sunlight, and he saw the hints of deep purple shimmer in the strands. He'd noticed them before, but this was the first time he felt free to touch the silky strands. His fingers sifted through the ends of her hair, enraptured by the change in the color.

"Right, brother?"

Jasper looked up to find Milo smirking at him, clearly amused by catching him off guard. He ignored him and whatever inane question he'd asked. There was no valet at Devil's Playground, so he grabbed Veronica's purse from the floorboard, handed it to her, and shut the door.

"Let's go inside and get checked in." Jasper slipped his hand around Veronica's and gently tugged her along with him. He liked the way her hand tightened on his for a moment, as though she was surprised he'd laced his fingers with hers.

Milo's smirk became a shit-eating grin as he followed them. "Since it's obvious you weren't listening, I'll repeat myself. I was telling Veronica that our family might be an eccentric bunch but they're a lot of fun."

Jasper grunted. "Maybe for you since you're as crazy as they are. But for me, they're—"

"Don't finish that sentence unless you want Mom to hear," Milo hissed over Veronica's head. "She's standing right inside the door."

"Shit," Jasper whispered.

Between them, Veronica giggled. He glanced down at her because he liked the sound.

"What?" Milo asked.

"Jasper told me a lot about your family this week. I think he's worried that you'll all run me off," she answered his brother. Then, she turned her face up to look at him, her brown eyes sparkling with humor. "I'll be fine. I promise. I've dealt with a lot of eccentric and even some mean clients. I'm sure your family is lovely."

"Famous last words," Jasper muttered as they walked through the open double doors to the lobby of the resort lodge.

Veronica laughed again.

"Jasper! My baby!"

He barely refrained from rolling his eyes at his mother's exclamations. She was calling his name as though it had been a decade since they'd last seen each other rather than a couple of days. They worked in the same office for fire's sake.

"Mom, I just saw you a couple of days ago at the office. Why are you acting like I'm returning from war?"

His mother huffed at him as she came closer. "Is that any way to talk to your mother?" she asked, sounding haughty and put-out.

"Yeah, Jas, is that any way to talk to—oof!" Milo's taunt was cut off by Jasper discreetly smacking him in the back of the head. "Hey! No need for violence. I don't need to be concussed on my wedding night. It'll ruin the mood."

His mother sighed as she came to a stop in front of them. "Can you two not behave for five minutes? And not act like such children in front of this lovely lady. You should be embarrassed. I know I am."

Milo and Jasper shared a look over Veronica's head but managed to keep from rolling their eyes.

"Now, are you going to introduce me or have you forgotten all the manners I tried to teach you over the years?" Leila Bayat asked.

"Mom, this is Veronica Salt. Veronica, this is my mother, Leila Bayat," Jasper said.

Veronica held out a hand to his mother. "It's wonderful to meet you, Mrs. Bayat. Jasper has told me so much about you."

Leila brushed her hand away and grabbed her by both shoulders, pulling her into a hug. "No need to be formal, dear. I'm so pleased to meet you." She released her, pushing her back just far enough to study Veronica's face. "Honestly, I thought Jasper was making you up to keep his meddling aunt from playing matchmaker this weekend until he called me a couple of days ago and told me to be sure there was an extra room for you at the lodge."

Veronica thought she heard Jasper mutter something about his aunt being less of a meddler than his mother, but she didn't want to react and get him in trouble.

Veronica didn't have time to respond because Leila glanced at Jasper, but didn't release her. "And speaking of that, Jasper, I'm afraid there is a problem with the room situation."

"What problem?" he asked, reaching out to hook his arm around Veronica's waist and pull her away from his mother and into his side. He squeezed her tighter when she let her weight rest against him, cuddling a bit closer to his body.

His mother's eyes moved over them as they stood together, and a faint smile tugged at her mouth. It vanished so quickly that Jasper wasn't certain Veronica saw it, but he did. And it made him suspicious as hell.

"There are no extra rooms this weekend," his mother said, forcing her face into the semblance of a frown.

He could tell it was fake because there was a line that appeared between her eyebrows whenever she was truly irritated, and it was missing. Leila the Meddler was striking again. "Mother..."

"I'm sorry, darling. It's just not possible. Now, if you'd told me you needed another room two months ago, I could have done it."

Jasper didn't bother arguing. He knew that she was digging in. "I'll just go speak to the manager myself, then."

Still holding Veronica against his side, he moved toward the counter, hearing his mother sigh behind them.

"Jasper—" Veronica began.

"It's fine. She's just playing matchmaker. I'm sure there are rooms left."

Veronica didn't say anything else, just did her best to match her stride to his. When he realized he was moving too quickly for her, he slowed down, his arm around her waist loosening a bit.

A tall, statuesque woman with blonde hair stood at the counter. Her nametag declared that she was the manager and her name was Poppy.

"Hello, Poppy," Jasper said when they came to a stop on the other side of the antique counter. "I'm here for the Bayat-Shah wedding this weekend. My mother was supposed to arrange for two adjoining rooms for us. She forgot to do so."

The woman's smile was serene. "Your name, sir?" she asked.

"Jasper Bayat."

She looked down at the computer screen in front of her and began typing. After a few moments, she looked back up, her face pulling into a gentle frown. "I'm sorry, Mr. Bayat, but we don't have two adjoining rooms available. Our last four rooms were booked about an hour ago. But I do have you in one of our cabins. It is one bedroom, but there is a pull-out couch."

Jasper glanced over his shoulder and saw his mother watching them, her arms crossed over her chest and her brows raised. The smirk playing about her mouth told him that this little hiccup was due to her scheming. He wouldn't put it past her to have reserved the last four rooms just to create exactly this situation.

Why was she so determined to make his life more difficult?

Jasper faced the manager again. "That will have to do. Could you please give me a call if there are any cancellations on a two-bedroom cabin or two adjoining rooms happen to become available?" He knew it was long shot, but he had to try.

"Of course, Mr. Bayat."

"Please call me Jasper," he stated. "I always look around for my father when I hear Mr. Bayat."

Poppy's answering smile was more genuine. "Of course. Let me get you checked in. Will you need two keys?" she asked.

"Yes, please."

As she began to type away, Jasper looked down at Veronica. "I am sorry about this," he said. "I asked my mother to take care of it earlier this week and it's clear that she didn't. I should have handled it myself."

Veronica tilted her head to look up at him. She seemed calm, but the blush was back in her cheeks. "It will be fine."

"I can room with my brother until the wedding," he offered.

"It will be fine, Jasper," she said.

The fine tension running through her told a different story, though. Jasper felt a sharp pain shoot from his jaw down his neck as he ground his molars together. His meddling mother was likely to fuck everything up if she didn't butt out. He would have to make himself clear this evening.

He would also talk to his brother about rooming together until

Saturday, no matter what Veronica said. She should be comfortable while they were here.

A few moments later, Poppy looked up from the computer. "You'll be in the Campfire Cabin. If you follow the drive to the right of the lodge, it will be the fourth cabin on your left. There is a golf cart parked beneath the carport beside the cabin. It will be yours to use during your stay." She slid a little paper folder across the counter that held their keycards. "The wi-fi is free and the password is listed inside there," she stated, gesturing to the small folder. "Will there be anything else?" she asked.

Jasper shook his head. "Do you need my credit card?"

"No, the rooms for the bridal and groom party have been taken care of by the bride's family. Please enjoy your stay."

Jasper suppressed the scowl that wanted to take over his face. The Shah's were a nice family, but Prema's mother, Darya, and his mother had been pressuring him to attend the wedding with Prema's younger sister, Jasmine. He'd tried to be polite in his refusal, but he worried that Darya and Jasmine would expect him to act as her escort during the wedding since they were paying for his cabin.

Jasper took the keycards, trying not to crush them in his fist. "Thank you."

He took a firm hold on his temper as he guided Veronica away from the counter. "I am so sorry," he repeated. "I know I warned you that my mother was a bit of meddler, but I wasn't expecting something like this."

"You think your mom is the reason there are no extra rooms?" Veronica asked, obviously bewildered. He understood her confusion. Most parents would never go to such extremes to get their way.

He glanced down at her, quirking a brow. "I inherited my determination to get what I want from my mother, and I can assure you, this was all her."

Veronica chuckled, which took him by surprise.

"You think this is funny?" he asked. As they walked out the front door, his mother and brother were noticeably absent. It was clear they had decided to escape while he was distracted by checking in.

"Not necessarily this...only at the idea that there is someone who might be more devious and pushier than you. And that it annoys you so much."

She was looking straight ahead, so she missed the way he looked at her, surprised that was her response. He knew he was a pushy, bossy, arrogant asshole. He just couldn't believe that Veronica was discussing those aspects of his character as though they amused her rather than upset her.

Maybe this weekend wouldn't become a disaster after all.

CHAPTER SEVEN

VERONICA WAS SHOCKINGLY CALM.

When Leila Bayat announced that Veronica and Jasper would have to share a room, nerves had erupted in her belly, threatening to overwhelm her. She'd been so distracted by the nervous anticipation gripping her that she'd almost missed the wave of smugness that came from his mother.

The sensation had brought her back into her head with a thud. Even with her mental shields firmly in place, Veronica could sense Leila's satisfaction with the situation. It seemed that Jasper wasn't the only member of his family who broadcasted his emotions without thought.

It was clear that Leila wanted them to room together. That she'd even taken steps to ensure that happened.

Milo's amusement washed over her as well, quickly followed by affection. It was clear that he was used to his mother's machinations and that he was enjoying his brother's plight.

Veronica decided then and there that she was going to go with the flow this weekend. It was clear that Jasper's family didn't resent her presence. In fact, it was obvious that his mother intended to play matchmaker. She deliberately ignored the little voice in the back of her head that said they might not feel the same once they discovered that she was an empath. If his mother and brother were anything like Jasper, they wouldn't decide that her abilities made her undesirable.

But if they did, Veronica was beginning to believe that it wouldn't matter to Jasper. That he made his own choices and wasn't the type to cave to pressure from his friends or family.

Jasper swept her along out to the car, and he insisted on opening the door for her again. He didn't say anything as he followed the drive in a wide circle back to the narrow concrete road that led behind the main lodge. Veronica noticed that his knuckles were white as he gripped the wheel, but he had his emotions locked down tightly. There wasn't even a whisper of anger or stress coming off him.

While she appreciated the effort he was making to keep his own mental walls up, she didn't want him to shut down completely. She didn't want him to feel the same kind of pressure that she felt when she was with a partner.

He stopped the car in front of the fourth cabin on the left, turning into the drive and pulling beneath the carport next to the golf cart. Before Jasper could open the door and climb out of the car, Veronica put her hand on his forearm.

"Jasper, I'm going to say something, but I don't want to upset you."

He turned to face her. "Whatever it is, just tell me. Don't worry about upsetting me. I'm a big boy and I can handle it."

Veronica took a deep breath. "Okay. I can sense that you've locked your emotions down tightly. I know it's because you don't want to overwhelm me, but I also don't want you to feel like you can't be yourself." She tilted her head, gazing into his eyes. "Does that make sense?"

"It does," he answered. "And you're right. I've been working on my mental shields, so you don't have to worry about protecting yourself from me. Just like you want me to be myself, I want you to be able to do the same." He laid his other hand over hers on his arm. "So, what are we going to do?"

Veronica shrugged. "I'm not sure. You're the first man I've ever dated that cared enough to try."

He suppressed the scowl that wanted to take over his face and focused on what she said. "Are we dating?" he asked.

That tell-tale blush worked its way up her neck to her cheeks again. "Um...well...I assumed after you kissed me that meant..." Veronica stopped speaking and cleared her throat, clearly uncomfortable. She dropped her eyes to the steering wheel, no longer looking at him.

When she tried to withdraw her hand from his arm, Jasper held it fast. "Look at me, Veronica." He could tell she didn't want to, but, after visibly steeling herself, she met his gaze. "If you're okay with it, we are dating."

"If I'm okay with it?"

"If it was completely up to me, the answer would be, yes, we're dating exclusively and seeing each other often. But I don't feel like I can make that decision on my own since consent is an important part of any relationship, so I need your agreement."

The embarrassment faded from her expression, replaced with a hesitant smile. "And if I agreed?"

"Then, you'll find out what it's like to date a djinn. I have to warn you, we can be intense, single-minded, and demanding. Some would even say overwhelming."

"I think I understand that already," she quipped back, her smile turning cheeky.

"Then, that's settled. We're dating. Which means you're stuck with me the rest of the weekend because my girlfriend isn't allowed to abandon me to my crazy family. I need your protection and support."

"Protection?" she sputtered. "How am I supposed to protect you?" She wasn't going to even think about the word *girlfriend* just yet. If she did, her hopes would soar too high, too quickly.

"If you're here, they won't try to set me up with their friends' daughters, cousins, or random women they meet on the street."

"Women they meet on the street?" she asked.

"They have no shame."

She couldn't control her answering giggle. She could also feel the relief emanating from Jasper. He was taking her at her word and relaxing his guard around her. It made her chest feel warm and light to know that he trusted her enough to do so. Strangely enough, his emotions weren't as heavy or sharp as they had been before. It was as if some part of him relaxed around her. She liked the idea. Probably too much.

"Well, are you ready to go inside and see what the cabin looks like?" he asked.

Veronica nodded.

It took them a few minutes to make it to the cabin because she argued with him about grabbing her own bags. He tried to insist that he would carry them, but she refused, stating that he needed to handle his own luggage, and she could handle hers.

When it became clear that she wasn't going to budge, Jasper relented and let her wheel her suitcase up to the door of the cabin, but he still carried her other bag along with his own. Though she rolled her eyes, she couldn't stop the smile that tugged at her mouth.

He gave her the key cards, stating that if she was going to be independent and sassy, she could open the door. Laughing again, Veronica did just that.

As soon as they entered, she stopped and stared. The cabin was small, but still beautiful. The walls were painted a soft white and the molding and trim throughout the open living area was a warm red oak, giving the space a cozy, almost old-fashioned feel. The living area was situated right in front of the entry and boasted a couch, a coffee table, and a flatscreen television mounted to the wall to their right. There was a small woodstove with a glass door in the corner to the right as well.

A small dining table was situated in the space directly between the living area and the kitchenette, already set with beautiful taupe stoneware that appeared to be handmade. With the art on the walls, the potted herbs above the kitchen sink, and the little touches throughout the space, the cabin exuded a homey, comfortable vibe that made Veronica want to curl up on the couch with a cup of tea or glass of wine, a book, and a small fire burning in the woodstove.

"Wow," she murmured.

"I know. That isn't a couch, it's a loveseat," Jasper commented as he carried the bags past her and turned to go down the short hall leading to what had to be the bedroom.

Veronica followed him, pausing in the doorway to the bedroom to take it in. A king-sized bed dominated the space, draped in a thick duvet the color of slate. Actually, it seemed larger than a regular king. Veronica studied it, trying to figure out exactly what size it would be considered. Since Devil's Playground catered to the paranormal community, she assumed it was scaled for supernaturals with larger secondary forms. Or huge humanoid builds.

There was a heavy black dresser against the wall to her left and two matching nightstands next to the bed. The walls were painted a pale gray that held a hint of blue. The drapes were open, allowing in the late afternoon sunlight, but Veronica could see that they were heavy enough to keep the light out when closed.

"Wow," she repeated.

Jasper set the suitcases on the floor at the end of the bed and dropped her extra duffle bag on the foot of the bed. "Yes, apparently all the rooms have Alaskan king-size beds."

"You could fit two bear shifters on that thing...in their bear form."

Jasper smirked at her. "I think that's the point."

Veronica shook her head. "Sorry, I've just never seen a bed that big before."

He chuckled. "Well, you'll be able to tell your friends that you've slept in the biggest bed you've ever seen after this weekend."

Veronica opened her mouth to tell him that he didn't need to sleep on the couch. The bed was so big they could both sleep in it and never know the other person was there. Before she could speak, his cell phone rang.

Shooting her an apologetic look, he pulled it out of his pocket. He sighed when he saw the screen. "It's my mother. I have to take the call."

"That's okay," Veronica assured him.

He lifted the phone to his ear and edged past her to leave the bedroom. "Hey, Mom. What's going on?"

Veronica didn't follow him, wanting to give him his privacy. She walked over to her suitcase and rolled it toward the open closet. She spent the next ten minutes hanging up her dresses and the nicer outfits she brought for the parties, lunches, and other gatherings. She'd been embarrassed by how much she'd packed until she saw that Jasper had a suitcase and a garment bag for himself.

She had just finished when Jasper appeared in the open door to the closet, startling her. "Ahhhh!" she yelled, tossing a handful of lingerie at him.

When she realized what she'd done, Veronica covered her mouth with both hands and stared at Jasper with wide eyes. A pair of silky turquoise panties were draped over his shoulder, and he held a lacy white bra in his other hand.

"Oh, my God," she gasped, rushing forward to grab her undergarments. "You scared me half to death!"

Moving quickly, she snatched the panties off his shoulder, the bra out of his hand, and bent down to sweep up the assortment of panties and bras she'd managed to throw in his direction. Without looking at him, she turned and dumped them all in her suitcase before she slammed it shut.

She knew her face had to be bright red because it felt hot enough to catch fire. When she turned back toward him, she covered her face with her hands and released a hysterical laugh.

"Um, you okay?" Jasper asked.

"Fine. Would you mind leaving the closet so I can die of embarrassment in peace and solitude?"

He chuckled. "I would apologize, but I don't mind women flinging their underwear at me."

"Oh, my God," she repeated. "Oh, my God."

A deep belly laugh interrupted her mumbling. Veronica peeked through her fingers to see that Jasper had thrown his head back as he guffawed. A smile trembled on her mouth, and she clamped her hands on it to keep from laughing aloud. His mental shields weakened, and she felt his amusement. She couldn't see it, but the emotion brushed against her skin, as light and effervescent as champagne bubbles.

There was also an undercurrent of affection. He genuinely enjoyed her. It wasn't something she often sensed from others. Dominique made it clear that she liked Veronica, but her mental shields were so formidable that not even a stray emotion escaped. Her parents loved her, but they were too worried about bombarding her with their feelings, so they always held themselves back. Just a little. Still, she felt that distance keenly.

This was the first time she'd felt such fondness and pleasure from a man she was dating. The thought took her aback, and Veronica dropped her hands from her face. How sad was it that not one of the handful of men she'd dated held such regard for her? She deserved more than that. Why hadn't she expected it?

Jasper came forward, mistaking her expression for more humiliation rather than an epiphany. His hands cupped her shoulders. "Hey, don't be embarrassed. If it makes you feel better, when I get back from helping my mother, I can throw my underwear at you. It won't be as colorful, but I'm willing to go all out and toss in my socks, too."

He pulled her in for a quick hug. Veronica couldn't help but laugh at his offer.

"I'll pass," she said. "I'm pretty sure my entire head would catch fire if you did that."

"Why?"

"Because if I blushed any harder, I would spontaneously combust."

He chuckled, his hand cupping the back of her head to tuck it beneath his chin. She felt the vibrations of his laughter against her cheek and heard the deep rumble of his voice as he spoke again.

"I have to go help my mother with an issue that's cropped up with the wedding. I shouldn't be gone too long. I'd bring you with me, but Mom would just turn you into another minion and order you around. Why don't you relax for a bit? Feel free to order whatever you want from room service. I'll take care of it before we leave. The party is in three hours and there will be food, but it's going to be appetizers and little desserts rather than a full dinner. Or we can order food when we get back to the room tonight."

Veronica wrapped her arms around Jasper's waist. She liked the way he tried to take care of her. "How about we order something after the party? Then, we can hang out and eat together."

"Sounds nice," he replied. His hands stroked over her hair where it fell down her back.

Veronica nuzzled him a second longer, liking the way he smelled and how his arms felt around her. Then, she stepped back. If she didn't, she would be tempted to stand there and let him hold her as long as he wanted.

"I'm going to take a nap. I'll get ready when I wake up," she said.

He studied her face, his hands still clinging to her hair. "Whatever you want," he said, a smile playing along his lips. "Knowing my mother, I won't be back until she has to stop whatever she's doing and get ready for the party." He didn't wait for her to reply, leaning down and pressing a quick kiss to her mouth. "I'll be back before it's time to head out though. I promise."

Veronica nodded, but didn't speak. She watched as he left the closet, lifting her hand to press the tips of her fingers to her lips. Though it had been brief, the kiss hit her in the gut. It was such a simple gesture, yet it meant more than he must realize.

No longer sure she could nap, Veronica decided to focus on unpacking her toiletries. If she stayed busy, she couldn't think too much about how Jasper made her feel.

CHAPTER EIGHT

"YOU HAVE GOT to be kidding me!" Jasper said as soon as he entered the suite his parents were staying in.

When he tried to turn around and walk right back out the door, he saw that his brother had already shut and locked it. Milo leaned back against the wood, crossing his arms over his chest, looking as though he didn't have a care in the world.

It was an ambush. Plain and simple.

Jasper turned to face his mother, who sat on the small sofa near the window. A charcuterie tray, a bottle of red wine, and four glasses sat on the coffee table.

"Come sit down, Jasper," his mother commanded, gesturing to one of the club chairs that faced the couch.

"No, Mom. You said you had an emergency with the wedding, so I rushed over here to help and it's clear that you don't need any help from me."

"Jasper, sit down. I want to know more about Veronica."

Knowing she wouldn't leave him alone until he did what she wanted, he sighed and flopped down in the chair facing her. A few seconds later, his brother mirrored his position in the chair to his left.

Wearing a prim expression, his mother filled the wineglasses exactly halfway and passed one to him and one to Milo. "Cyrus, my love. Get in here and drink your wine."

"I told you that I didn't need to be involved in this conversation," he called back. "I can learn what I need to know by speaking to the young woman. There's no need to interrogate Jasper."

His mother rolled her eyes and sighed. "Cyrus, get your ass in here now!"

Though his father was in the other room of the suite, Jasper could hear his heavy sigh. There was a rustling sound, probably the newspaper, and a grunt, then his father appeared. He trudged toward the couch and accepted the glass of wine his wife held out to him, staring down into it.

"You don't think this conversation calls for whiskey?"

"Zip it, Cyrus."

"Leila, you just—"

"Zip. It."

Jasper lifted his glass to his lips and drank half of it in one gulp. Swallowing, he picked up the wine bottle and poured more. "You get five questions. And I can choose not to answer two."

"Ten questions and one abstain," his mother shot back.

"Seven questions, two abstains. Final offer."

His mother knew him well enough to understand that he wasn't bluffing. If she didn't agree, he was out of here. Their gazes locked and fired, but he wasn't backing down.

Finally, she sighed again. "Agreed."

Negotiations over, Jasper leaned back in his chair. "Go ahead."

"How did you meet?"

"Milo didn't tell you?" he asked her.

His mother's lips pressed together hard. "He didn't even tell me he knew the name of your date until this morning. And he said it was Veruca. Not Veronica."

Milo snickered until Jasper backhanded him. "This isn't the set of Willy Wonka."

"I know, brother, but her last name is Salt. I couldn't resist."

Jasper rolled his eyes at his brother's juvenile attitude.

"Well?" Leila asked. "Are you going to answer my question?"

"I met her at Mystical Matchmakers."

"Oh, is she one of your matches?"

"Is that one of your questions?" Jasper answered.

His mother glared at him, her mouth hardening into a firm line. "Yes."

"No, she isn't one of my matches. She works there."

His mother's mouth fell open. "And she's dating a client? That's... that's..."

Jasper sat up and set his glass on the table. He leaned forward, resting his elbows on his knees and stared hard at his mother. "I asked her out three times. She turned me down all three. She said it wouldn't be professional to go out with a client. It wasn't until I told her that she would be my date to the wedding or need to refund my fees that she agreed. And that was only after her boss gave approval. You will not give her a single ounce of shit about this. Am I clear?"

His mother gaped at him. They often butted heads because they were so similar, but this was the first time he'd ever taken such a hard line with her. He kept his gaze on hers until she finally nodded.

"Okay, then," she continued. "Third question—"

"Actually, this is your fourth."

Milo tried to stifle his laugh, but the muffled sound still escaped. Leila shot him a dark look that promised retribution.

"Based on your reaction, it's clear you really like her," Leila said. "How long have you been dating?"

"A week."

"A *week*?!" his mother exclaimed.

Jasper picked up his wineglass and drained it before setting it back on the coffee table. "That was your fifth question and I'm abstaining from the final two."

Leila pointed a finger at him. "You are not. None of this seven-question bullshit. You've only been dating for a week, but you're willing to throw down with me about this woman. What am I missing?"

He rubbed his hands over his face in exasperation. Why couldn't he date someone without having to play twenty questions with his mother? Why couldn't he just enjoy Veronica's company without having to justify or explain it his family?

"Jasper, seriously. I'm worried about you. You never rush into anything. You're always planning ten steps ahead for anything in your life—whether it's work or dating or even where you're going on vacation. Yet you seem incredibly serious about this woman in a week. It's unlike you and I want to understand."

He let his hands fall away from his face.

"Just tell her, brother," Milo said.

Jasper looked at his dad, who nodded at him. "You were right, Dad," he admitted.

His father smiled but didn't say anything else.

"Right about what?" Leila asked, looking between her husband and two sons.

Jasper turned back to his mother. "Dad always told me that I would know when I met the right woman. The woman for me. That I would see her and never want to look away. Since the moment I met Veronica, I haven't wanted to look away."

"Just like I don't want to look away from your mother," Cyrus said.

Leila looked at her husband, eyes soft. "You said that?"

"I've told you that, wife," Cyrus replied. "Repeatedly."

Her eyes narrowed. "Yes, you've said that to me. As you should. I didn't realize you also said it to our boys."

"Of course I did," Cyrus said. "How else would they know when they met the one?"

Leila's eyes went wide, and she turned back to Jasper. "She's the one?"

Jasper held up a hand like a traffic cop. "Wait just a damn second. Do not get too excited." When she visibly wilted, he sighed. "She is the one, Mom, but like you pointed out, we've only been dating a week. Veronica is shy and introverted. I can't come on too strong with her or she'll run away. It's taken me six weeks to get to this place with her. If I go about this the wrong way, it could take me months to win back her trust. If I'm even able to."

His mother nodded enthusiastically. "I understand."

"And you both need to tone it down a bit this weekend," Jasper continued, pointing to both his mother and brother.

"What did I do?" Milo asked.

His mother just gasped in affront.

"I'm serious, Mom. I know you're curious about her, but don't fawn all over her. And for the love of God, don't tell her that she's the one!"

"I would never," his mother said, pressing a hand to her chest.

Jasper and Cyrus shared a look of commiseration.

"I won't!" she insisted.

Hoping she meant it, Jasper turned to his brother. "Milo, I know you live to give me shit, but I don't want you to include Veronica in it. She's an only child and she's shy. She's not used to dealing with family dynamics like ours. The way we bickered when we got here made her tense. I could feel it. So, for the weekend, take it easy. Give her time to get used to us."

For once, his brother wore a serious expression. "I won't do anything to make her uncomfortable," he agreed. "And I'll do my best to keep our more...eccentric relatives in line around her."

Jasper smiled at his brother. "Thank you."

"I'm sorry," his mother interrupted.

Surprised, Jasper turned toward her, his brows near his hairline. "What exactly are you apologizing for?"

His mother's expression was sheepish. "About the room. If I had realized..." She didn't finish her sentence, shrugging.

Knowing she would never outright admit that she hadn't bothered to arrange for another room, Jasper sighed and let it go. "It's okay. There's a pull-out couch. I'll be sleeping on it this weekend." He rubbed his hands over his face, missing the devious gleam that flashed in his mother's eyes. "There is something I need to talk to you about Veronica, though. Normally, I would let her tell you herself and in her own time, but I'm going to need your help and understanding this weekend so I'm giving you a head's up."

His mother nodded, sipping her wine.

"Veronica is an empath. She's usually upfront with people about it, so it's not a secret. I know she wanted to tell you herself, but I'm circumventing that, so you need to keep it under your hat. She's used to people treating her differently when they find out. And people often feel like she's going to invade their privacy because of it. Or at least that's what she thinks."

"I won't tell a soul without her permission, and you know it won't affect how I treat her." Jasper believed the second half of her statement, but not the first. Leila could be discreet when it came to business dealings, but family gossip? He didn't quite believe her.

"How is she going to do this weekend with so many people here for the wedding?" Leila asked.

"That's what I wanted to talk to you about. She said she should be fine, but that sometimes she gets tired from shielding so hard. I'm going to keep an eye on her. We'll go back to the cabin or find an empty room if she's getting overwhelmed or fatigued. So, don't give me, or her, any shit about it. Okay? She'll feel badly enough."

His mother's eyes twinkled. "Oh, I won't give you shit. Maybe if you spend enough time in your room, I'll get a grandbaby sooner rather than later."

Jasper rolled his eyes and looked to his brother and father. "You need to keep your tempers in check. And keep your mental shields up."

On the whole, the entire family was fiery and fierce. They tended to lose their tempers quickly and easily. There were often shouted disagreements at any family event, quickly followed by hugs and back-slaps, because the conflicts burned out as fast as they flared. His father and brother were often guilty of starting them and then standing back to watch the mayhem that ensued.

Milo, for once, didn't give him a sarcastic response. He just nodded.

His father, on the other hand, said, "I don't know why you're telling me this. Your mother is the one who loses her temper the most." He gestured to his wife.

Leila smacked him on the arm. "Cyrus!"

Jasper leveled a look at his dad, which had the older man grinning and saying, "Okay, okay. Best behavior."

They chatted for a bit longer about the weekend and the party that evening. Jasper teased his brother about having such a circus for a wedding since the itinerary was a full page long, which meant his brother socked him in the bicep. When he mentioned that the party was starting in two hours, his mother went into a tizzy and all but ran them out of the room, stating she would need every bit of that time to get ready.

Jasper was glad because he'd been thinking about Veronica almost constantly since he entered his parents' suite. He wondered what she was doing. If she was able to take a nap and rest. If she was taking a bath. Which led to his thoughts to the image of her naked. Not the place his mind should be when he was talking to his parents and brother.

He headed back to the cabin, careful to be quiet when he entered. The space was silent when he entered. No television or music playing. He walked through the living room and glanced down the short hall, seeing that the door to the bedroom was open. The room was dim, and he could see the edge of the bed, but nothing else.

Had she left?

His heart rate sped up, as did his steps, as he moved down the hall. When he reached the door to the bedroom, he stopped. She was lying on her side on the far side of the huge bed, her back turned to the door, which was why he hadn't seen her from the hall. She didn't turn to look at him, so he crept around the bed.

Veronica was asleep, her hands tucked beneath her cheek like a child. Her face was relaxed in sleep, peaceful and beautiful. He hated to wake her, but he wanted to be sure she would have plenty of time to get ready.

Unsure of how to wake her, he moved to the bed, settling on the side. His hip fit in the curve of her body, brushing against her knees. She sighed, but didn't open her eyes. Not wanting to startle her, he reached out and trailed his fingers across her cheekbone, brushing a few strands of hair away from her face.

"Veronica," he murmured. "It's time to wake up."

A small smile curved her lips, and she shifted, rolling more onto her back. Her eyes opened, their warm brown depths sleepy and soft. "Hey," she sighed. "You're back."

Her lips curved into a smile as her hand came up to cup the back of his hand where it rested on her cheek.

Unable to resist the pull of her lips, Jasper leaned over and pressed his mouth to hers. The hand on the back of his moved to his face, her fingers brushing his jaw. A low sound vibrated in her throat as she kissed him back. Those fingers moved to the back of his head, weaving into his hair. Her lips moved against his, opening so the tip of her tongue could touch his upper lip.

Though he wanted to take the invitation to deepen the kiss, Jasper lifted his head. Her cheeks were flushed now as she looked up at him, the sleepy expression still on her face, but her eyes sparkled with pleasure. Seeing her like that, Jasper realized that he wanted to kiss her, gentle and sweet, every day for the rest of his life.

"I'm sorry to wake you," he said. His voice was rough, so he cleared his throat. "But the party is in a little less than two hours. I wasn't sure how much time you'd need."

She started to sit up, so he scooted back, giving her space. "Yeah, I should probably get going." Veronica hesitated. "Do you need to shower or anything before I take over the bathroom?"

He shook his head. "It takes me about twenty minutes to get ready, even for something like this."

With a shy smile, she got to her feet and leaned over to kiss his cheek. It was only the second time she'd done it, but he wanted it to become a habit. He was breaking through her reserve, getting past the walls she erected between herself and other people.

Now, he had to show her that she wouldn't regret it.

CHAPTER NINE

VERONICA SMOOTHED a hand down the lavender dress she wore. The halter dress had ruching down one side of the bodice, starting just below her breasts and ending at mid-thigh. The gathered seam meant that the hem was higher in that spot, baring most of her right leg. The curving hem was several inches longer around the rest of the garment. The stretchy purple material was shot through with silver thread, giving it a metallic sheen. The color made her pale skin glow and brought out the deep purple highlights, courtesy of her fae heritage, in her long hair. Nude peep toe pumps sat at the end of the bed, waiting for her to put them on. She'd left her hair down, curling the ends, and kept her make-up soft and shimmery.

She'd been hesitant about the outfit all week, only bringing it because Dominique insisted she should. Jasper had been in the shower when she went into the closet to slip on the dress and finish curling her hair.

But when he came out of the bathroom, they'd both stopped and stared at each other. Veronica had swallowed hard at the sight of him. The simple black shirt and slacks shouldn't have taken her breath away. Every time she saw him when he came into Mystical Matchmakers, he wore a suit and looked hot as sin.

Tonight, he wore something more casual and somehow that was even more attractive. The cut of the shirt emphasized the breadth of his shoulders and the narrowness of his waist. His hair wasn't perfectly styled as usual, but rather messy and falling over his forehead.

"You look beautiful," Jasper said, staring at her from his place by the bathroom door. His bare feet were silent as he walked toward her.

"Thank you. You look very handsome." Her reply was soft, mostly because all she could hear at the moment was the pounding of her heart.

He stopped in front of her, staring down at her face. Neither of them had put on their shoes yet, so he towered over her. "I like your hair down. The color is beautiful."

Veronica felt her cheeks heat and knew she was blushing. "I don't often wear it like this."

"I like it," he replied, his gaze moving over the curtain of hair falling around her shoulders. He reached out and lightly grasped one of the curls.

"Thank you." She shifted awkwardly, unsure of what to do or say next.

He released her hair but didn't move. Veronica blinked, unsure of why he was still standing there, staring down at her.

Finally, he smiled and said, "I need to get my shoes out of the closet."

Veronica startled, realizing she was standing right in front of it. "Sorry."

She moved out of the way, blushing fiercely. Veronica slipped on her shoes and transferred her phone, ID, debit card, and a lipstick over into a small nude clutch that matched her shoes. By the time she was done, Jasper had emerged from the closet and put on his socks and shoes.

"Are you ready?"

At Jasper's question, she looked up to find him watching her. "I am."

"Do you have a wrap or jacket?" he asked. "It's chilly outside."

She smiled at him. "I do."

After she grabbed the pashmina she brought, Jasper drove them to the main lodge and parked the golf cart in the special spots for them by the entrance. The lobby was strangely empty as they walked inside with only two lodge employees standing behind the antique counter where Jasper checked them in.

But it soon became clear where everyone was when Jasper led her down a hall to their left. The low strains of jazz music drifted out of the open double doors at the end of the hall. Veronica could hear the hum of conversation as they drew closer.

"I'll stick close to you," Jasper murmured as they approached the doors. "Introduce you to everyone."

"You don't have a creepy uncle, or anything do you?" Veronica asked, only half joking.

"None of them are creepy but they are all annoying."

She couldn't hold back the giggle that erupted from her mouth at his words. Before she could ask him to remind her how many uncles he did have (he'd told her, but she couldn't remember), they were inside.

The room had been transformed into a romantic lounge. Floral arrangements of varying sizes were placed all over the room and in the center of the tall round tables scattered around. Despite the variety of species, each flower was a shade of red ranging from bright crimson to a deep burgundy. Flameless candles flickered in small votives on every flat surface. There were two bartenders behind the heavy, ornate bar, both busy mixing drinks. Three waitresses worked the room, carrying drinks to people at the tables. In each corner of the lounge, there was a table full of finger foods.

While the space wasn't packed with people, it was crowded enough to make Veronica hesitate. There were so many emotions and ideas flying around. Though she couldn't usually read individual thoughts, she could sense it when someone was thinking intently.

Taking a deep breath, Veronica fortified her mental shields, building them to a thickness that pushed out all the emotional static that a large group of people tended to give off.

"Let me find Milo and Prema and I'll introduce you," Jasper said.

As he looked around, Veronica spotted his mother standing in the center of the room, her arm threaded through the arm of the man standing next to her. He could only be Jasper's father, considering he looked exactly like him, just a little older.

As soon as Leila saw her, a wide smile broke out across her face. She turned back to the couple she'd been talking to, her mouth moving quickly, and then tugged her husband away a few moments later. The woman was bearing down on them, all but frog-marching her husband in their direction.

"Um, Jasper—" Veronica murmured.

Before she could figure out how to tell him that his mother was all but sprinting toward them, he saw her as well. Despite the background noise, Veronica heard his put-out sigh.

Leila Bayat stopped just in front of them, that same wide grin still pulling at her mouth and her dark grey eyes shining. Veronica could feel the happiness wafting from the older woman. And the excitement.

Suddenly, her nerves lessened because it was clear that Jasper's mom was very excited about her youngest son getting married. It was difficult to be nervous when someone was all but beaming at you with sheer joy.

"Veronica, you look so lovely," Leila said, releasing her husband long enough to grasp Veronica's shoulders and pull her in to kiss her cheeks. When she released her, Jasper's mother gestured to the man standing beside her. "This is my husband, Cyrus."

Blinking in shock at the warmth of Leila's welcome, Veronica turned toward the handsome older man and held out her hand. "It's so nice to meet you, Mr. Bayat," she said.

Cyrus smiled at her, gently cradling her fingers with his as he lifted the back of her hand to his lips for an old-fashioned kiss. The move surprised a laugh out of her, especially when he threw in a wink.

"Call me Cyrus, please," he insisted. "If you're putting up with my son for the weekend, we're certainly on a first name basis."

Another laugh escaped her as Jasper scoffed at his father's antics.

She almost jerked when his arm slipped around her waist, tucking her against his side, and his hand rested on her hip.

Though he clearly wanted to remonstrate his father, all he said was, "Dad."

Cyrus smirked at his son. "You were right, Jas. She's way out of your league."

Veronica opened her mouth to speak, unsure of what in the heck she could say to that, but Jasper merely shook his head at his father.

"Stop flirting with my girl, Dad," he said. "Now, where are the bride and groom? I wanted to introduce Veronica to Prema."

Her nerves had faded during the brief conversation with Jasper's parents, but they returned full throttle at the mention of his brother and his soon-to-be sister-in-law.

"I think they snuck out to neck in the coat closet," Cyrus answered, twisting his head to peer around the room. "I know that's what I'd be doing if your mother wasn't such a spoilsport."

Leila whirled on her husband, already chastising him. Jasper didn't bother to intervene, just guided Veronica away from his bickering parents.

"Sorry about that," he murmured. "I know I warned you what my family was like, but it's different seeing it in person."

When he looked down, she was smiling up at him. "Your parents are hilarious," she insisted. "And fun. It's also clear that they adore each other."

Jasper was tempted to lean down and press his lips to the small dimple that had popped up in her left cheek, but he suppressed the urge. "They do adore one another, but I think their love language is annoying each other."

Veronica's laugh was unrestrained as she tilted her head back. It was from her belly and shook her entire body. "That's what makes them funny and fun," she replied.

"Maybe to you. To me, it's frustrating as hell."

She laughed again, unable to help herself. During the short time she'd worked with Jasper at Mystical Matchmakers, he'd come across as intense. And as a workaholic.

But this week, she was seeing a different side of him. He was both sweet and snarky, making her blush one moment and laugh the next. In truth, it made her wonder why he needed the matchmaking service at all. Though he was blunt, there was nothing off-putting about Jasper. He was handsome, successful, witty, and clearly a devoted son. Why hadn't some other woman snatched him up yet?

Jasper left his hand on her lower back, guiding her across the room. People tried to speak to him, but he lifted a hand and waved as he kept them moving until they stopped right in front of Milo, who was standing next to a stunning woman in white. She appeared to be close to Veronica's age.

The young woman was smiling up at Milo and Veronica could feel the love and happiness radiating from her. It made Veronica smile as well. The young woman, who must be Milo's fiancée, Prema, turned and all but hopped in excitement when she saw Jasper and Veronica.

"Brother-in-law!" she cried. She stepped forward and threw her arms around Jasper's neck. He gave her a hug in return.

"Hey, now. Keep your paws off my fiancée," Milo complained, wrapping an arm around the woman's waist and tugging her away from his brother.

Laughing, she allowed herself to be pulled away from Jasper. Her light brown eyes were bright as she looked toward Veronica. "Hi, I'm Prema Shah."

"Soon to be Bayat," Milo interrupted.

Veronica took the hand that Prema held out and shook it. "Veronica Salt."

"So nice to meet you, Veronica," she said. "I'm glad you came with Jasper. I thought my mother was going to set him up with my sister, Jasmine, and I was afraid she'd eat him alive." Prema laughed, but her affection for her sister radiated from her.

"I'm glad I came with Jasper, too," she murmured. At her words, Jasper's hand slid down her lower back around her waist, pulling her deeper into his side. She glanced up to find him looking down at her, a slight smile on his face.

Veronica relaxed as they chatted, finding that she liked Prema. She clearly loved Milo and fairly sparkled with excitement as they discussed the wedding. After a while, she realized that she was letting Jasper take some of her weight, leaning deeper into him. When she tried to straighten, he held her tighter, keeping her body against his.

For the next hour, he kept her close. He either held her hand or kept his arm around her waist as he introduced her to his family members and friends of his parents. He got her a glass of wine and plate of snacks before finding them a quieter corner table so they could eat the finger foods. She felt his attention, knew that he was keeping track of whether she was tired or not.

Maybe his high-handedness should have irritated her, but, honestly, Veronica appreciated it. He was taking care of her. It had been a long time since someone tried to do that. None of her previous boyfriends had, that was for sure.

Throughout the evening, Veronica noticed a pretty young woman watching her with Jasper. She looked enough like Prema for Veronica to assume they were related. Until she got a closer look at her eyes. They were light brown, almost gold. The same as Prema's. Veronica realized that she must be Prema's sister, Jasmine. There were waves of irritation and frustration surrounding her. And jealousy. She wondered if Jasmine had been hoping that her mother set her up with Jasper after all.

It wasn't until Jasper approached an older couple speaking to the young woman that her suspicion was confirmed.

"Darya, Darius, this is Veronica Salt. My date for the weekend," Jasper said.

The woman smiled and took both of Veronica's hands in hers. "Hello, dear. Your dress is beautiful!" She released Veronica's hands, turning to the young woman. "This is my daughter Jasmine, Veronica."

Jasmine didn't hold out her hand, but she did nod at Veronica.

Chuckling, Darya patted her daughter's shoulder. "Isn't it lovely, dear? You don't have to pair up with Jasper this weekend after all."

Another wave of jealousy and irritation wafted from Jasmine and

Veronica realized that the young woman definitely was upset that she *wouldn't* be spending time with Jasper this weekend.

Feeling awkward, Veronica shifted on her feet, trying to take a small step away from Jasper. She didn't manage it because he tugged her closer, looking down at her.

"Do your feet hurt?" he asked. Before she could answer, he turned back to Darya, Darius, and Jasmine. "Please excuse us. We'll see you all at the luncheon tomorrow."

He basically dragged her away from them. She assumed he was going to find her a place to sit down, so she stammered, "Really, Jasper. My feet are fine. I don't need to sit down."

"Good."

That was all he said as he lifted his chin in the direction of his brother and then followed that with a nod to his parents. Then, he snaked his way through the crowd of people and right out of the lounge.

"Um, what are we doing?" she asked.

"You're tired. We're going back to the cabin."

Veronica was at a loss for words again and started stammering. "I, um, but...Jasper—"

He didn't stop moving until they reached the lobby. "Wait here for just a second," he said.

Before Veronica could utter another incoherent syllable, he walked toward the counter and spoke with one of the resort employees. The woman he spoke to nodded along and began writing down whatever he was saying. After a few moments, she smiled at him, still nodding. Jasper took a folded bill out of his pocket and handed it to the employee. What was he doing?

Veronica realized that she was more exhausted than she'd thought because she couldn't even form the question when Jasper returned to her side and began walking toward the front doors of the lodge. She shivered as the cool night air hit her arms and pulled the soft shawl closer around her upper body.

It wasn't until she was seated in the golf cart, and they were on their way back to their cabin that she was able to speak again.

"What were you talking to the desk clerk about?" she asked.

Jasper zipped down the gravel path beside the main lodge, making Veronica's breath back up in her throat and her heart pound in her chest. She reached out and grabbed the bar that ran across the front of the golf cart's dashboard.

"Just ordering us some food. It'll be to our cabin shortly."

The chilly night air was breaking through the fog of fatigue. Veronica finally said, "We didn't have to leave, Jasper. I was still doing fine."

He shot her a sideways glance. "Your knuckles were turning white around the stem of your wineglass, and you were getting quieter and quieter. I could tell you were getting tired."

Warmth grew in her chest. He'd noticed all that? Still, it made her uncomfortable. "I don't want your family to be upset with you because of me," she argued.

"I warned my parents and Milo that we would probably leave early, so this was no surprise to any of them. They were fine with it."

"What about the rest of your family? They're going to think I'm rude."

"They won't know we left because of you. They're used to me disappearing in the middle of family gatherings. They know that big groups of people and small talk aren't my thing. If anything, they'll think I'm being rude."

Veronica took a deep breath. She understood that he was trying to be considerate of her, but she also didn't want him to unilaterally make decisions for her. "How about next time, you ask me if I'm getting tired or if I'd like to leave? As opposed to dragging me out of the room like a toddler in need of a nap."

He chuckled at her words, which made her shoot him a narrow-eyed stare.

"Okay, okay, no need to bring out the death glare," he said.

Veronica rolled her eyes and crossed her arms over her chest, trying not to shiver. In the moving golf cart, there was no protection from the January night. In this part of Texas, it rarely got below freezing, but it did get much cooler when the sun went down.

"You're right. Next time, I'll ask you if you're ready to leave. Or flat out tell you that I'm the one who wants to go," he agreed.

Veronica cocked her head as she studied him. "You wanted to leave, didn't you?" she said.

Jasper smirked at her as he pulled beneath the small carport that housed the golf cart at the cabin. "Yes, I did. I could see you were beginning to get tired and decided that was more than enough reason to step out early."

She rolled her eyes as she climbed out of the golf cart. "Why didn't you just tell me you wanted to leave? I wouldn't have argued."

"I'm telling you now."

Veronica sighed and decided to stop bickering with him. It was a useless endeavor. Plus, they were already back at the cabin. He unlocked the door and opened it for her, allowing her to enter first.

"Why don't you change first?" he asked. "I'm going to get the pull out situated while we wait for our dinner."

She nodded, ready to be out of her dress. When she emerged from the bathroom ten minutes later, her face freshly washed, hair wound up in a messy bun, and dressed in comfy lounge pants and a t-shirt, she found Jasper smoothing a blanket over the mattress of the pull-out couch.

"I thought we could sit on this and watch a movie or something while we eat," he said. "That way we could put our feet up."

She smiled. "That sounds nice."

Jasper grinned back at her and plopped down on the mattress, propping his right foot on his left knee and tugging at the laces of his dress shoes. An ominous creaking sound came from the bed, followed by the high-pitched screech of metal against metal. Jasper's feet flew up into the air as the mattress beneath him collapsed with a crash.

Veronica rushed forward and knelt next to the destroyed bed. "Oh, my God, Jasper. Are you okay?"

He pushed himself into a sitting position. "I'm fine."

She bit her bottom lip, trying very hard to suppress the wild urge she had to laugh. "Are you sure?"

He studied her before he asked, "Are you trying not to laugh?"

Veronica pulled her upper lip between her teeth too, fighting to keep the muscles of her face still. Since she didn't trust herself to speak without giggling, she shook her head.

He sighed and tried to stand up. The mattress beneath him shifted, nearly throwing him off the other side of the bed. His arms and legs went flying as he rolled sideways.

Veronica couldn't hold it in any longer. A small snort escaped her, then another. Finally, she couldn't control the laughter. She rolled back onto her butt, wrapped her arms around her waist, and rocked back and forth as she guffawed.

Jasper fought his way to the side of the mattress and basically rolled onto the floor on his hands and knees. The sight of him all but crawling off the broken bed set her off into loud whoops. She covered her mouth with both hands as tears ran down her face, but she couldn't stop.

When he got to his feet, Jasper reached down, grasped her wrists, and tugged her to her feet.

"I-I-I'm sorry," she said. "It's not funny. Y-y-y-you could have been hurt."

He gently pushed her away from the bed, folded it back up, and jammed it back into the cavity in the sofa. "I'm fine. Though I'm beginning to rethink my belief that you were a sweet, innocent woman."

Veronica covered her face with her hands and snorted again, her shoulders shaking. "I could have told you none of that was true," she managed to wheeze.

The doorbell chimed, echoing throughout the small cabin. Hoping it was the food he'd ordered, Jasper left Veronica giggling and snorting behind her hands and went to the door.

By the time he'd collected the bag containing their food and tipped the man who'd brought it, she more or less had herself under control.

"I really am sorry I laughed at you," she apologized again.

Jasper shrugged. "Didn't hurt my feelings," he replied. "And it was funny. But I suspect it won't be so funny when I have to call the front desk for a rollaway bed."

She frowned. "Oh, no. I can do it."

"No, I'll do it while you set the food out on the coffee table."

Veronica studied the couch, her expression thoughtful. "How about we eat on the bed in the bedroom? I'm ready to prop my feet up and the bed sounds more comfortable anyway."

Surprised by her suggestion, Jasper nodded.

"Good."

Veronica took the bag and carried it into the bedroom while he headed toward the phone on the kitchen counter. Before he called the front desk though, Jasper took out his cell phone and texted his mother.

> Jasper: I'm onto you.

The business with the pull-out falling apart had his mother's meddling written all over it. Djinn were notorious as pranksters and grudge holders. He didn't doubt that his mother's scheme was for them to share the bed.

> Mom: I have no idea what you're talking about.

Shaking his head at his mother's reply, Jasper put in a call to the front desk, asking for a rollaway bed and explaining what happened with the pull-out couch. The clerk said someone would be at the cabin shortly with one.

By the time he was off the phone, his mother had texted again.

> Mom: What happened?

> Jasper: You made the pull-out bed fall apart in my cabin.

> Mom: No, I didn't.

> Jasper: 😑

Mom: I really didn't.

Jasper knew that his mother would have admitted it, so there was only one other option. He texted his brother.

Jasper: Nice magic, Milo.

Milo: Thnx. What did I do?

Jasper: You broke the bed on the pull-out couch in my cabin.

Milo: No, I didn't

Rather than arguing with his brother, Jasper tucked the phone back in his pocket. His brother had to be lying. He was the only other person in his family who would mess with Jasper this way.

He was about to walk to the bedroom when the phone on the counter rang. Curious, he picked it up.

"Hello?"

"Mr. Bayat?"

"Yes?"

"This is Luna at the front desk. I'm so sorry. I'm afraid we have no rollaway beds available."

"What?"

The clerk cleared his throat. "All the rollaway beds have been given out. I'm afraid we don't have any more available."

Oh, Jasper was going to kill his brother. He'd let him enjoy his honeymoon with his new bride, but when he came back, he was a dead man.

"Thank you," Jasper replied. He replaced the phone receiver and put his hands on his hips, staring down at the counter.

He was still standing there, trying to calm himself down, when he heard the soft tread of Veronica's bare feet on the wood floor behind him.

"You okay?" she asked.

"Fine. Just trying to figure out if I want to risk sleeping on the loveseat as it is or dragging out the mattress for the pull-out and sleeping on the floor."

"Why?"

"Because the hotel is out of rollaway beds," he answered. "Those are my only options."

"No, they're not."

Jasper turned to face her, confused. "There aren't any extra rooms or beds, so it's either what I mentioned or sleeping in my car."

Veronica shook her head, lacing her hands together in front of her. "You can sleep in the bed with me. It's big enough for both of us plus a few other people."

She smiled slightly as she said it, amused at the gargantuan bed.

"I don't want you to be uncomfortable," Jasper argued. "I'll be fine on the floor."

"Well, I won't be fine with you on the floor. Just sleep in the bed. Unless it'll make *you* uncomfortable..." She twisted her fingers together. "If it would, I'll sleep on the couch. I'm a lot shorter than you. I wouldn't have any trouble fitting on it."

"You won't sleep on the couch," Jasper stated, his tone downright bossy.

"Then, it's settled. You're sleeping in the bed."

She didn't give him a chance to argue, just disappeared back down the hallway to the bedroom.

Tilting his head back, Jasper studied the ceiling and wondered exactly how long he might end up in prison after he killed his brother. Because Milo was definitely a dead man walking.

Jasper was going to torture him first though because sleeping in that huge bed with Veronica and keeping his hands to himself was going to be agonizing.

CHAPTER TEN

VERONICA WOKE IN STAGES. She was warm and cozy on the most comfortable bed she'd ever slept on.

Though she was halfway tempted to let herself drift back to sleep, she opened her eyes and blinked several times. Jasper's face was only a few inches from hers, his eyes closed and his breathing deep and even. He didn't look younger in sleep. But he did seem much more peaceful. With his eyes closed, she wasn't distracted by the intense, nearly black color of his irises or the way he looked at her as though he could read her mind.

He was so handsome that her fingers tingled with the need to touch him to see if he was real. As she continued to look at him and listen to him breathe, Veronica could no longer resist. Her fingers trailed over his brow bone and down to his cheek. His skin was so hot, as though fire burned within him.

At her touch, his eyes opened and locked on her face. His gaze was warm and still sleepy as he looked at her. The intensity that usually surrounded him was at rest. Looking at Jasper right now, Veronica was no longer intimidated. He looked like the kind of man she could fall in love with.

The urge to kiss him came out of nowhere. Veronica couldn't stop herself from looking down at his mouth. A low rumble emerged from his throat, and she decided to stop holding back. With his words and actions yesterday, Jasper made it clear that this weekend wouldn't be the last time they saw each other.

Veronica inched forward, her gaze moving from his lips to his eyes. They stared at each other as she closed the distance. She sensed he wanted to let her decide if she would kiss him or not.

When their lips touched, his hand glided up her arm to the base of her neck, slipping beneath her braid to curve his fingers around her nape. It wasn't until his mouth opened against hers, that Veronica thought about the fact that she had morning breath.

Inhaling sharply, she started to pull away. "Let me brush my—"

Before she could finish her sentence, he rolled, pulling her on top of him, and his mouth found hers again. Veronica forgot about morning breath, about her insecurities, about the world in general. All her mental shields came crashing down at the sensations. She could feel the pleasure he took from the kiss. The arousal that poured through him. Or maybe that was hers. She couldn't tell.

Jasper wrapped her braid around his fist, tugging her head back to bare her throat. He kissed just below her ear before his mouth moved to the place where her neck and shoulder met. The light scrape of teeth made her shiver and Veronica rocked against him, her knees parting to dig into the mattress on each side of his hips.

His mouth moved back to hers, his tongue sliding into her mouth. His free hand moved to her ass, pressing her tighter against his body. Veronica felt the hard length of his dick beneath her and her breath caught in her throat. He liked what she was doing, she could feel that.

Jasper released his hold on her braid, his hand moving down her back to the hem of her t-shirt. Hot fingers slipping beneath the cotton and branding the flesh of her side. She shivered at the rough scrape of his palm against her ribs. When his hand cupped her breast, his thumb brushing over her nipple, Veronica gasped against his lips. Her body shuddered as she panted against his mouth.

Her reaction seemed to break the spell forming over them. Jasper's lips eased on hers, his kiss becoming lighter and more teasing. His hand returned to her braid, tugging it lightly until she tilted her head back. He pressed another kiss to the side of her throat, wringing another shiver from her.

He released her hair, and Veronica lowered her chin so she could look at him again.

"Good morning," he murmured, his voice low and rough.

Another shudder ran through her muscles, which made him smirk at her.

"Good morning," she replied.

They stared at each other in the morning light. He was smiling and relaxed, more than she'd ever seen from him before. She thought that she could stay right here for the rest of the day. But only if he stayed with her. Unfortunately, she knew it wouldn't be possible.

"What's on the agenda today?" she asked.

"The groomsmen are playing golf this morning and the bridal party is having a spa day." He paused. "I made you an appointment for a few treatments when my mother asked me about it. I know you don't really know Prema or anyone else, so I made sure your treatments would be after theirs. I wanted you to have some privacy, so you wouldn't be tired before the dinner tonight."

She continued to stare down at him, taken aback that he'd gone to so much trouble for her.

When she didn't say anything, he continued, "Or you can come play golf with me and go to the wedding rehearsal after or just hang out in the room or at the indoor pool. There's a luncheon today, but most of the wedding party won't be there. It's more for the family to have a chance to visit with each other before tomorrow. Do whatever makes you happy."

Whatever made her happy?

She hadn't thought about what made her happy in a long time. Veronica started to shift off him, but Jasper's hands clamped onto her hips, holding her still.

Finally, she asked, "What spa treatments did you book for me?"

He grinned up at her, his thumbs massaging her hipbones through her shorts. "A facial, a sauna session, and a massage."

An answering smile spread across her face. "I think I'd like to do that, especially if it's just me."

"Good."

Jasper looked so satisfied that she laughed. She realized that her mental shields were down, that she'd never put them back up after the kiss. All she sensed from him was peace.

Her surprise must have shown on her face because he asked, "What?"

"You're so peaceful. I don't even need to shield myself from you," she answered. "It's nice to be able to let my guard down."

His smile faded and his hands clutched her tighter. His usual intensity returned as he stared up at her. "You make me calmer. Being near you eases the chaos in my mind. I'm usually as loud and quick-tempered as the rest of my family, but you...you bring out something inside of me that I've never felt before. I like who I am when I'm with you."

Her stomach clenched. "I don't want you to change for me."

That was the last thing that she wanted. She liked what she was learning about Jasper. And she knew what it was like to have the person you were with want you to change. It hurt.

He shook his head. "I'm not changing for you. I'm changing *because of you*." His hands slid up to her shoulder blades, tugging her down until their faces were a few inches apart. "I like it."

He kissed her and, once again, Veronica felt his pleasure and his sincerity. He released her mouth and rolled them over so that she was beneath him.

"I don't want you to be anything but who you are, Veronica," he said. His hands brushed stray strands of hair from her face. "I'm learning more about you every day and I like what I know so far."

She nodded and he kissed her one last time before he levered himself off the bed. She blushed when he adjusted his erection in his lounge pants but didn't take her eyes off him as he picked up the phone.

Glancing at her, he asked, "What do you want for breakfast? And you like coffee, right?"

"Something light. Toast or fruit. I'm not very hungry in the morning. And I do like coffee, but with cream and sugar."

He nodded and pressed a button on the phone. A few moments later, he placed an order for croissants, fruit, bacon, and a pot of coffee. There was a single-serve coffee machine in the kitchen, but there weren't many pods.

They took turns in the bathroom and Veronica took a minute to wash her face and brush her teeth. When she emerged, breakfast had arrived. The service at Devil's Playground was top-notch, that was for sure.

Glancing at his watch, Jasper said, "I need to shower. Are you done in the bathroom?"

Veronica nodded and took a bite of bacon as he disappeared inside the bathroom. Thank God she was done with her light breakfast when he came out fifteen minutes later. The door opened with a puff of steam that carried the scent of his soap. Jasper emerged in nothing but a white towel wrapped around his hips.

If she'd been eating, she would have choked at the sight of him. His arms, shoulders, and chest were roped with thick muscle. Hair covered his pectorals and taut belly. Veronica swallowed hard because her mouth was watering at the sight of him. His black hair was damp and messy, and he hadn't bothered shaving the scruff on his cheeks. He could have stepped out of the pages of one of the romance novels she liked to read.

She tried not to gape as he walked into the closet, giving her an excellent view of his bare, muscled back and round backside covered by the towel.

Veronica grabbed the neck of her t-shirt and fanned it, trying to cool down. Was it suddenly hot in the cabin?

Jasper came out of the closet with a stack of clothes in his hands. He tossed them on the end of the bed and pulled a pair of black underwear off the top. She couldn't control her eyes as he stepped into them and pulled them up beneath his towel. Her gaze followed his movements until she realized what he was doing, and she forced herself to look down at the coffee cup in her lap.

A second later, she heard the towel hit the floor and the blood rushed to her face. Dear God, he was standing less than five feet in front of her in nothing but his underwear. The temptation to look at him was intense, but she didn't dare. At least not until she heard the rustle of fabric followed by the sound of a zipper.

She glanced up and found herself staring into Jasper's black eyes as he shook out a t-shirt. Veronica could barely breathe when she saw the heat in his stare. He tugged the shirt over his head, breaking the intense eye contact and covering his torso. Veronica couldn't help one last glance at his chest before the fabric fell over it. He followed the t-shirt with a light sweater. She supposed he would need it if the groomsmen were going to play golf this afternoon.

Jasper's hair was messy from pulling on his shirt. He ran his fingers through it as he came around the bed and sat down next to her hip. Veronica let him take her coffee cup, watching as he put it off to the side.

"Look at me," he murmured.

She did as he said. He leaned closer, placing his palm on the bed on the other side of her body, bringing his face a few inches from hers

"Your spa appointments are at two o'clock this afternoon. We should both be done by five-thirty and we'll have the evening free."

Technically, that was a lie. There was another family event—a dinner—but he'd already told his parents that he wasn't coming or bringing Veronica because she needed to be rested before the wedding since they would need to be in attendance most of the next day.

His free hand came up to push a few strands of hair away from her cheek. "I'd like to have dinner with you tonight. Just you and me. Is that okay with you?"

Veronica nodded. "That sounds really nice."

"Really nice?"

Her cheeks warmed but she smiled. "I'd like to spend the evening with you."

"Better," he murmured. His hand moved from her hair to her cheek, holding her head steady as he leaned forward. He kissed her, a light, gentle caress. Her breath was a warm flutter against his lips as he pulled back. "Enjoy your day, Veronica."

She couldn't suppress the shiver that ran through her when he said her name. She knew he felt it because his eyes heated and his fingers slipped back into her hair, tugging lightly at the strands.

"I'll see you tonight."

When he kissed her again, his lips opened over hers and their tongues tangled, slow and wet. Veronica lost herself in the kiss, her hands coming up to clutch his shoulders. The shudder that ran through her was larger this time. Tingles rushed over her scalp and down her spine, settling between her legs.

She was panting when they parted, her lips swollen and hot. Part of her wanted to tug him back onto the bed and tell him to finish what they'd started this morning, but the rest of her was still hesitant. As much as she wanted Jasper, her previous experiences hadn't been all that great. She'd managed an orgasm with one of her boyfriends during sex, but most of the time, she'd been unable to let herself go and enjoy what was happening between them. She'd been too intent on keeping her mental shields up and the effort and thought it required meant that she couldn't allow herself to fully immerse herself in how her body felt and any pleasure she might be experiencing.

"I'll see you in a few hours," Jasper whispered.

"Okay."

Veronica listened to him leave the cabin, her entire body humming with arousal. She understood then why his touch and his kisses had affected her so deeply. She didn't need her mental shields with him. Not anymore.

The question was—what was she going to do now?

CHAPTER ELEVEN

VERONICA DIDN'T THINK she'd been this relaxed in her entire life.

She spent the morning working, ate a light lunch, and then drove the golf cart to the main lodge for her spa treatments. Jasper had left it for her, which she appreciated.

Her spa treatments had been like heaven on Earth. She wasn't sure how Jasper managed it, but the aesthetician who gave her a facial had been one of the most Zen people she'd ever been around. Her emotions weren't shielded, but her thoughts were calm and gentle, like soft waves against the shore of a lake.

The massage therapist was completely different. Her mental shields were solid. Not a single stray emotion leaked through. The utter silence of the room and the long, slow sweeps of the therapist's hands on her skin had put her in a state of deep relaxation. She hadn't felt so at ease in her skin in years.

The feeling of peace stayed with her on the trip from the main lodge back to the cabin. She didn't run into anyone else on the short drive. She still had twenty minutes before Jasper was due back from golf, so she took the time to put on a little make-up and fix her hair.

She was just coming out of the bathroom, trying to figure out what she should wear on her first *official* date with Jasper Bayat, when she heard the door the cabin open. Smiling, she emerged from the bedroom to see how his day had gone but stopped short when she saw him.

"What happened?" she asked, rushing forward.

Jasper limped over to the sofa and plopped down on it. His sweater was ripped at the shoulder, carried streaks of dirt, and bits of grass and crushed leaves. His pants weren't much better. His left pant leg had one long stripe of mud down the side. His shoes were muddy, too.

"My brother shoved me, and I fell down a hill into a mud puddle," Jasper groaned, letting his head fall back to rest on the couch.

Veronica's eyes latched on to the muddy scratch on his throat. It was mostly a raised red welt, but there were a couple of places where the skin had broken and there was blood gathered.

"Milo *shoved* you?" she asked, anger welling up inside her.

Jasper opened one eye to look at her, a rueful smile on his face. "Well, in his defense, I kinda deserved it. I *might* have moved his golf ball. More than once."

Veronica rolled her eyes. She was still irritated, but now with both men rather than just Milo. "Why do you and your brother fight like that?"

He shrugged, closing his eyes again. "Part of our relationship has been fighting like cats and dogs."

"I never understood that saying," Veronica said. "I had a cat and a dog growing up and they never fought. They snuggled up together every night."

Jasper chuckled and lifted his head. "Djinn usually have an affinity for certain elements. In our family, we're drawn to fire. It influences our personalities. The Bayats tend to be intense, fierce, and short-tempered. We also like to argue and fight. It's fun to us. Like I told you, family gatherings tend to get loud and confrontational. We're not usually violent, but none of us back down when someone challenges us."

"And this explains why you and your brother fight like two pre-teen boys? Because it's *fun*?"

He shrugged again. "Yes?" His answer was a question rather than a statement.

With another eye roll, Veronica moved over to the couch. "Okay, let's get you into the bathroom so you can clean up."

There was a bench in the shower. Jasper could wash off in there.

Jasper pushed himself to his feet, keeping his weight off his left foot. Veronica pointed to it. "And what happened there?"

"I twisted my ankle when I fell. It's not broken, but I'm afraid we won't be able to go out tonight."

"That's fine," Veronica said. "We'll order room service again. That was nice last night."

Veronica sensed his disappointment, but to be honest, she liked the idea of having him to herself tonight.

She grabbed his left arm, lifted it up so it went around her, and shoved her shoulder into his armpit. "Lean on me and I'll help you to the bathroom."

Jasper looked down at her. "You look really pretty."

Veronica tried to fight the blush that rose in her cheeks, but it was a losing battle. The way he looked at her and the things he said to her made her feel as giddy and awkward as a schoolgirl.

She got him into the bathroom and asked him what clothes he wanted for after his shower. He asked her to grab his pajama pants, a pair of underwear, and a t-shirt out of his suitcase. When Veronica came back into the bathroom, Jasper had already stripped out of everything but his black boxer briefs. She wasn't even taken aback by the sight of him nearly naked because the huge bruise on his left shoulder and the scrape down his spine made her freeze.

"Jasper, your back," she gasped.

He grunted. "It's already healing, I promise. I'll be good as new in a few more hours."

Grumbling under her breath, Veronica left his clothes on top of the closed toilet, which was only a couple of feet from the shower. She asked if he needed help, but he said no, so she left the bathroom. But she did linger just outside the door, listening as he turned on the shower. She waited until he was finished, and she heard him climb out before she left the bedroom. Veronica was worried that he would fall in the shower, but when she was sure he would be okay, she went into the kitchen. After a little digging, she found a Ziploc baggie, a kitchen towel, and plenty of ice in the freezer.

By the time Jasper made his way out of the bathroom and settled onto the bed, a pillow crammed behind his back, she'd returned with the ice pack. His brows raised when he saw what she'd brought.

"I'm healing fast, Veronica," Jasper argued. "I don't need an ice pack."

She totally ignored him, grabbing one of the extra pillows from the head of the bed and propping his foot up with it. With a sigh and a faint smile, Jasper didn't try to stop her as she laid the towel over his swollen left ankle and then arranged the baggie of ice on it.

"There. We'll leave this for ten or fifteen minutes. It may be healing fast, but this will still help the process along," she said, putting her hands on her hips. She noticed the scratch on his forehead. "Did you disinfect that cut?"

He shook his head. "I washed my face in the shower. That should be enough."

Veronica went into the bathroom and dug the mini first aid kit out of her toiletry bag. When she came back into the bedroom with it, Jasper winced.

"That's not necessary," he stated. "I washed it out well when I took a shower. And I'm a djinn. We heal fast. And don't get infections...much."

She gave him a dry look. "Don't be a baby. It needs to be cleaned out or it'll scar. Even if it doesn't get infected."

"Scars are sexy," he said, leaning away when she sat down on the bed beside him.

Veronica held back a laugh. "It'll only sting for a second. I promise."

With a put-out sigh, he sat up and let her dab the cut with an alcohol pad. He hissed at the sting, and she leaned forward to blow on it.

"You know you're just blowing germs into that, don't you?" he murmured. He leaned a little closer, his nose almost touching her throat. "You smell good."

She ignored his statement about germs, dabbing the cut again, but shivered when he leaned even closer, and his lips brushed her neck. "Thanks. It's probably the massage oil the therapist used."

"Hmmm."

Goosebumps broke out over her arms and legs as the low hum he let loose vibrated against her skin.

"Are you hungry?" she asked, her voice little more than a whisper.

"Starving."

"What do you want for dinner?"

His arms came around her, one wrapped around her shoulders and the other low on her back, just above her hips. "Are you on the menu? You smell good enough to eat."

Veronica couldn't help the giggle that escaped her because his lips moved against her throat as he spoke, and it tickled.

"I suppose that was a cheesy line," Jasper admitted, releasing her, and leaning back against the headboard.

"Maybe just a little," she agreed. "But your lips tickled when you were talking."

His answering smile was warm and a little tired. "Honestly, I'd love some pasta."

"That sounds good," Veronica agreed. "There're two different kinds on the menu. Wanna order both and share?"

"Sounds good." Before she could get up, Jasper caught her with a hand around the back of her neck, pulling her in for a kiss. "Thanks for taking care of me."

"Anytime."

After Veronica tossed the alcohol pad in the bathroom trash, she picked up the phone in the kitchen and ordered their dinner. She also requested a bottle of wine, salad, and dessert. Just because they couldn't go out for their date didn't mean they couldn't have a date in the cabin. She would pay for the room service meal before they checked out since she added so much food to it.

As with breakfast, the meal was delivered almost preternaturally fast. Veronica had no idea how the restaurant here at the resort was able to make and deliver the meals so quickly, but she wasn't going to complain.

She carried the baskets containing their food and the bottle of wine into the bedroom and found that Jasper had gotten up and ditched the ice pack into the bathroom sink.

"You weren't supposed to get up yet," she said.

"My ankle is much better. It'll be healed by the time we're done eating and watching a movie. I promise." He started to get up. "Let me help—"

"I've got it," she insisted, carrying everything over to the nightstand. "I ordered salad and wine, too. I'll pay you back for that."

"No, you won't."

"Jasper—"

"No, you won't," he repeated, his tone firm.

With a sigh, Veronica unpacked the food, pleased to see that there was a foil package containing garlic bread. Before she could talk him out of it, Jasper was on his feet, the bottle of wine in his hand.

"There's a corkscrew in the kitchen. I'm going to open this and grab some glasses."

Resigned, Veronica watched as he limped out of the bedroom. By the time he returned, she had the containers opened and sitting on the rolling tray she found in the closet.

He insisted that she pick the movie since he rarely had time to watch television or follow the releases. When she paused on a romcom that she'd been wanting to watch, he told her to go ahead and pick whatever. The trailer began playing automatically and he watched it while he sipped wine.

"Are you sure?" she asked. "It's what most men would consider a chick flick."

Jasper shrugged. "It looks funny. Let's do it."

They sat on the end of the bed and ate dinner off the tray while they watched the movie. When they were done with their food, they pushed the rolling tray to the side and scooted back on the bed, sitting side-by-side with their backs against the headboard. After a few minutes, Jasper shifted, putting an arm around her shoulders.

"This okay?" he asked.

"Yes," she murmured, resting her head on his chest.

He tugged her closer until she let her weight rest against his side. Veronica soaked up the contact. It had been a long time since she'd been held like this. Yes, he'd climbed into bed with her the night before, but they hadn't been touching when she woke up.

This was different. She was aware of the firm muscled length of his body, the heat of his skin soaking through her pajamas, and the slow, steady beat of his heart against her cheek. Though she was still relaxed from the spa treatments, a low hum of arousal began in her blood. It had been so long since anyone had touched her with more than platonic affection that just cuddling with Jasper affected her more than she expected.

"Thank you again for scheduling the spa treatments for me," she murmured. "The ladies wouldn't even let me tip them. They said it was taken care of."

"You don't have to keep thanking me," he replied, his fingers gently running through the ends of her hair. The movement tugged at her scalp and tingles spread from her head to down to her neck. "Did it help you relax?"

"I'm more relaxed than I've ever been."

She could hear the smile in his voice when he said, "Good."

Hesitant, Veronica lifted her hand, pausing for a moment before she finally placed it on the center of his chest, just next to her cheek. Immediately, Jasper's free hand came up to cover hers, pressing it closer. She tilted her head back, pulling away slightly.

He looked down at her, his dark eyes soft as they met hers. She loved the way he was looking at her. As though there was nowhere else he would rather be. Without thinking, she moved her hand, cupping his cheek. As she lifted her chin, Veronica pulled him toward her.

His lips were hot and felt like a brand against hers. That heat spread throughout her entire body. It was only their second day here and none of this felt fake anymore. The way he looked at her, the way he treated her, it reflected his true emotions. He liked her. He wanted her.

And the way he made her feel wasn't false either. She was falling for him. It was too fast, too frightening, but she wasn't sure she could stop it even if she wanted to.

Veronica opened her mouth when his lips parted over hers and a low hum escaped her at the touch of his tongue against hers. Jasper deepened the kiss by degrees, taking his time as though he would have been satisfied just to kiss her all night long.

But that wasn't enough for her. Not tonight. Veronica shifted, turning her body further into his. Jasper cradled her against him, but she wanted to be closer. She brought her leg around, placing a knee on each side of his hips, straddling his lap.

Jasper tangled his hands in her hair, holding her closer. His lips moved from hers, over her jaw and down to brand the side of her throat. She rocked against him, feeling the hard length of his erection beneath her.

The mental shields he'd built around his mind cracked, letting some of his emotions leak through. Veronica's breath caught in her throat. They were like a gossamer thread, so thin that it shouldn't have affected her. But they did, because as tiny as the leak in his shields was, it had the same strength and honed edge as a scalpel. It stole her thoughts and her control.

He wanted her with an intensity that matched her own. He ached with it, just as she ached. He took pleasure in her touch and in touching her in return. His own desire fed hers. It was unlike anything she'd ever experienced before. Veronica was swept along the wave of his emotions, her muscles winding tighter as though her entire body was hot and on the verge of melting.

Jasper's hands clasped her hips, holding her still, and his mouth left the skin of her neck. "Veronica, I don't want you to do something you'll regret."

"I won't."

His dark eyes remained locked on hers, as though he were trying to read her mind. Or at least determine her level of honesty with herself. His hands gripped her hips tighter, bringing her closer. "I need you to be sure because this will change things."

"How?"

"You'll have to be open to the idea that this isn't pretend. That you're dating me. That we're in a relationship."

She leaned back a little so she could see his face clearly. "I know it's not fake anymore. I believe what you said before. About wanting to be with me."

"I have a confession to make," he said.

Veronica froze as she felt a thread of worry worm through his mental walls. "What?"

"It was never fake for me."

She blinked at him. Once. Twice. Three times. "I'm sorry. What?"

"I never wanted for you to pretend to date me. I wanted you to actually date me," he admitted. "But every time I asked you out at Mystical Matchmakers, you shot me down and held me at a distance. None of the matches you found me worked out because they weren't the woman I wanted. They weren't you."

She didn't know what to say to that.

"It probably makes me an asshole, but I used the situation to my advantage, hoping that you would open up to the idea once we spent some time together. If it hadn't, I wouldn't keep pushing because I do understand the word no. I just felt like you were seeing me as a client and not a man and I wanted a chance to change that."

"It was never fake for you?" she asked. "Truly?"

He shook his head. Veronica could sense that he was worried she would be angry. But that he also didn't feel guilty about it at all.

Veronica knew she should be upset, that what he'd done was manipulative and underhanded. But she knew that he was right. She never would have given him a chance if he hadn't pushed her into a corner by insisting that she attend the wedding with him.

And she would have missed out.

CHAPTER TWELVE

JASPER STARED up at Veronica's face. Her thoughts were racing, it was obvious by the distant look in her eyes. But she didn't look upset. No, she looked as though she were considering his words carefully. It was something he admired about her. She didn't have kneejerk reactions. She listened. She weighed her thoughts and actions. She was calm and collected.

Those were Veronica's strengths, and they balanced out his tendency to bulldoze his way to his goals and his quick temper. Her empathy and compassion reminded him to consider the emotions of others. He often developed tunnel vision and didn't consider that his words or actions might trigger a response in the people around him. It wasn't intentional. He could admit his tendency to be a selfish asshole, but more often than not, when he fucked up, it was because he was oblivious. Without trying, she reminded him to be aware of how he affected those around him.

"What happens after the weekend is over?" she asked.

"The same thing that happened before we came here—we text, we talk, and we spend time together."

Her hands cupped his face, thumbs tracing the lines of his cheekbones. "We saw each other nearly every day this week."

He tugged her closer. "I know. I wanted to see you every day. Is that a problem?"

Relief streamed through him when she shook her head. Her hands slipped down his throat to his shoulders. Veronica pressed him back against the headboard as she lowered her head. He remained still, letting her come to him. It was difficult to do when his instinct was to go after what he wanted. That part of his nature was powered with the same fire that created his magic as a djinn. The same fire that gave him the ability to bend reality if he wanted it badly enough. Or if someone wished for it aloud in his presence.

Veronica's lips touched his and Jasper groaned at the taste of her. Her hands smoothed down his chest to the bottom hem of his shirt. Her nails lightly scratched his abdomen as her fingers slid beneath the fabric. He inhaled sharply at the contact. Her skin was cooler than his, but he wanted her to touch him anywhere she wanted.

He also wanted to touch her the same way. Jasper let his hands move up her back, beneath her t-shirt. The skin of her back was smooth and soft under his fingertips. She felt like satin beneath his hand.

Veronica surprised him when she straightened and tugged his shirt up until he lifted his arms and let her strip it from him. This time, when her hands moved over his chest, her delicate fingers trailed over his bare skin. Her eyes were locked on the movement of her hands on his body.

Then, she leaned forward and pressed her mouth to his throat. Her lips and tongue moved down his neck to his collarbone. Jasper held himself back, wanting to let her lead, but his hands flexed on her hips. She sighed, lifting her head.

Her cheeks were flushed, and her eyes were heavy-lidded as she looked down at him. "Do you want to stop?" she whispered. Her voice was shy, completely at odds with the desire on her face.

"No. Do you?" he asked.

Veronica shook her head, lifting her hand to place it in the center of his chest. "I'm a little nervous though."

"Why?"

She swallowed hard. "It's been a long time since I've trusted a man enough to…" She stopped talking, her hand flexing against him.

"But you trust me?"

Veronica nodded.

"Do you trust me enough to follow my lead?" he asked.

"Yes."

Forcing himself to move slowly, Jasper moved his hands up her spine from her hips to between her shoulder blades. She didn't resist as he pulled her down until he could kiss her. As their mouths meshed and he tangled his tongue with hers, Jasper felt her muscles relax against him. Veronica gave him more of her weight, leaning into him.

He slowly lifted her shirt, giving her time to change her mind or stop him, but Veronica raised her arms above her head, allowing him to remove it. A cotton bra covered her breasts, but he could see her tight nipples beneath the thin fabric.

Jasper smoothed his hands up her ribs, stopping just below her breasts. His thumbs brushed the band of her bra, moving back and forth slowly. He could see her pulse pounding at the base of her throat. Veronica took a shaky breath, her hips shifting. She gasped when her pussy ground against his cock.

He ran his tongue across the top of her breast until he reached her sternum. He pressed a kiss to her breastbone, feeling the way her chest rose and fell with pants. He could hear the catch in her breath when he ran his thumb over her nipple.

Jasper wanted to strip her naked and put his hands and mouth all over her. He was greedy for the smooth glide of her skin beneath him. But he held back. She was nervous and she'd admitted it had been a long time since her last relationship. He didn't want to overwhelm her or push her too hard, too fast.

He wanted her with him every step of the way.

Pulling back, he looked up at her face, running a finger down the edge of her bra. "I want this off."

She surprised him by reaching behind her and releasing the clasp herself. The bra fell from her body into his lap. Jasper swept it aside before he cupped her breasts, lightly running his thumbs over her nipples. Veronica's hands fisted in his hair when he took one in his mouth, curling his tongue around the tip before sucking lightly.

She rocked against him then, her weight coming down on his cock. He could feel the heat of her pussy through the pajama pants she wore. Releasing her nipple, Jasper held onto her and rolled until Veronica was beneath him.

Her long dark hair spread out over the pillows as she looked up at him, her eyes glazed with need. He wanted to picture her just like this from now on. The aloof demeanor she wore like a cloak was gone. She looked at him like she needed him more than she needed her next breath.

Jasper ran his hands over her abdomen to the waistband of her pajama pants. She didn't wait for him to ask, just nodded, her hands joining his to shove them down her hips. He stripped the cotton from her and tossed the garment to the floor. She wore only a pair of lavender panties edged with cream lace. He traced the scalloped edge of the waistband, watching as goosebumps erupted on her thighs. He liked that she reacted so strongly to his touch.

His fingers moved down, cupping her between her thighs. Veronica reached for him as she spread her legs, her fingers running over his chest and down his torso. Her hands paused, her nails lightly scratching his stomach when he rubbed a finger over her pussy. The fabric of her panties was damp and hot.

Jasper moved his hand, slipping it beneath the lacy garment until his middle finger encountered the slick, soft skin of her pussy. Veronica gasped as he pressed his palm against her clit and slid that finger inside of her. He thrust another finger inside of her, stroking slow and deep.

"You feel good," he murmured. "Wet and tight."

Veronica's only response was a moan, her head falling back, and her hand slid down his abdomen, leaving four small welts on his skin. He liked the sensation, but even more, he liked that she'd done it without thinking, her body reacting to his touch without thought.

When he moved his hand to strip the panties off of her, Veronica's eyes shot to his, but she didn't hesitate to lift her hips, letting him remove them and leave her completely naked.

She sat up, her fingers curling around the elastic waist of his pants. "I want these off, too."

Her words surprised him again. She'd been hesitant and nervous before, but now she was telling him what she wanted. And she was watching him with intense eyes as he shoved the pants and his boxer briefs off. Her gaze locked on his cock before she looked up at his face.

"I want to touch you."

"Anywhere you want."

He nearly jerked when her hands landed on his legs, just above his knees, and her palms slid up his thighs. Veronica squeezed his quads slightly, massaging the tense muscles beneath her grip. Jasper forced himself to remain still as her eyes and hands both focused on his cock.

Veronica licked her lips as her fingers ran down the length of his erection. She curled her fingers around him and stroked, tightening her grip as her hand moved. Jasper let her explore until, gritting his teeth against the sudden need to come, he put his hand over hers.

"Did I hurt you?" she asked, that hesitant expression returning to her face.

Jasper shook his head, gently removing her hand from his cock. "Just the opposite. I'm trying not to embarrass myself."

Veronica looked at his dick again as though she wanted to see him come. Jasper laced their fingers together, lifting her hand above her head as he came down on top of her. Veronica's free hand lifted to grip his shoulder as she wrapped her legs around his hips.

At the first touch of his cock against her pussy, her thighs tightened around him, as though she wanted to hold him closer. Jasper rocked his hips, feeling the bud of her clit against his erection. Her fingers dug into his shoulder as she matched his movements.

Jasper could feel how wet she was for him. He reached down, sliding a finger over her clit and down to her entrance, gently pressing inside. She arched her body, lifting her hips to meet his touch.

"You're ready for me" he stated. Then, he remembered. "Condom. We need—"

"I have an IUD.," she murmured. Full-blooded supernaturals couldn't carry diseases, something they were both aware of.

"Are you sure?" he asked, his body tensing over hers.

She nodded. A gasp escaped her mouth when he gripped his cock and lined it up with her pussy, slowly pushing inside her. When her body resisted, he pulled back and pressed in again. Little by little, he worked his length into her body until he was completely buried inside her. Her muscles clenched around him, her pussy growing wetter as he moved inside her, his pace slow.

Jasper released her hand and rested his weight on his elbows as he lowered his head to hers. Their lips met and she sucked his tongue into her mouth. He groaned as her hands tangled in his hair, tugging the strands.

He shoved an arm beneath her, cupping the back of her neck, and thrust into her harder. Jasper released her mouth, using his tongue to trace a line down the side of her throat before he nipped the side of her neck with his teeth.

Her panting breaths came faster as he angled his hips, his cock sliding against her clit with each stroke. Veronica moved with him, her pussy gripping him tighter and tighter. He wasn't going to last much longer. She felt too good. But he'd be damned if he came before she did.

Jasper raised his head, looking down at her. "Touch your clit for me," he demanded.

A bright flush worked its way from her throat to her cheeks, but Veronica did as he commanded, her hand leaving his hair to slip between their bodies. The tips of her fingers brushed his cock as she circled her clit.

Her body clamped down on his cock and he ground his teeth together. A bead of sweat dripped down his spine as he fought the urge to explode.

"Come for me, baby," he murmured, lowering his head and sucking her nipple hard.

Her fingers moved faster, but Jasper had to slow his thrusts. He paused, his dick buried deep inside her and groaned as he felt her muscles twitching around him.

"You're so close, aren't you?"

Veronica made a sound low in her throat, a cross between a whimper and a moan, and her pussy grew tighter and wetter. Jasper withdrew until he was barely inside her before he slid home again, going as deep as he could.

He kept his thrusts measured and used his mouth to tease her nipples, licking and sucking as she writhed beneath him.

Suddenly, her body went rigid, and she yelped. Her pussy clenched him so tightly that he had to fight the urge to move inside of her, the rippling of her muscles pushing him over the edge.

With a deep groan, Jasper kissed her, thrusting his cock into her faster and harder, riding her through her orgasm even as he came so hard that it nearly hurt. Their tongues tangled as the pleasure crested and began to recede.

Finally, Veronica's body relaxed beneath his, trembling every few moments from the aftershocks of her climax. The kiss grew gentler, softer, as Jasper stilled, letting his weight pin her to the mattress. She didn't complain. Her muscles seemed to melt into the bed beneath them.

He drew back, brushing her hair away from her face as he looked down at her. For the first time, Veronica's expression was completely unguarded as she met his gaze. She looked relaxed and languid.

"You're beautiful," he murmured, pressing kisses to her jaw and her eyelids when they fluttered shut.

"I was thinking the same thing about you," she whispered.

He grunted, which made her smile.

"I'll get up in a second," he said. "I'm not sure my legs will work yet."

A soft laugh escaped her. "Don't rush on my account. I like where I am."

"So do I," he agreed. "I always do when I'm with you."

Her eyes opened to study his face.

"What?" he asked.

"It always surprises me when you say things like that. Especially since you really mean them."

"I wouldn't say it if I didn't mean it," he countered.

Her hands smoothed down his back, as though she sensed that her words upset him, and she wanted to soothe him. "I'm beginning to understand that about you. I like that you say exactly what's on your mind. There's no conflict between the things you say to me and the emotions you feel. That's part of the reason I feel so peaceful around you."

The tension in his body faded at her words. "I like that I bring you peace. I want you to be happy."

Her dark eyes peered up at him, something vulnerable in her gaze. "I'm happy here with you."

As he dropped his mouth to hers, Jasper vowed to himself that he would do everything in his power to always make her feel that way.

CHAPTER THIRTEEN

VERONICA LAY BENEATH JASPER, relishing the weight of his body on hers. The heat of his skin against hers. She soaked up the contact like a dying plant soaked up water and sunlight. It had been so long since she'd been touched like this.

Jasper eventually withdrew from her and disappeared into the bathroom. He came back with a washcloth and gently pressed it between her legs. Heat flooded her face as he cleaned her up. When she tried to do it herself, he just stared at her until she lowered her hand back down to the mattress.

When he returned to the bed, Jasper gathered her close, slipping an arm beneath her head and bringing her right leg over his hips. She was practically draped over his side like a blanket. She relaxed into him as his fingers drew a line up and down her spine.

Veronica felt safer than she ever had before. Even with her parents, she'd always been on edge, always worried about upsetting them. It was so difficult for her trust others, yet Jasper was rapidly convincing her to trust him.

That was why his words took her off guard when he said, "I'm cancelling my membership to Mystical Matchmakers on Monday. I'm no longer in need of your services."

Veronica stiffened, suddenly wary.

He hooked a finger beneath her chin and tilted her face up so he could look at her. "I don't need another match. I found the one I wanted as soon as I walked in the door."

God, he had to stop saying sweet things like that. Every time he did, Veronica felt hopeful that this time things would work out. That he wouldn't ghost her the way other men had.

"Why did you get so tense?" he asked.

Veronica sighed. "I guess I'm waiting for the catch. I know it's my issue. You've been nothing but honest and great. There's no reason for me to automatically think the worst of the situation." She shrugged. "I'm used to the men I date thinking I'm too much work."

Jasper traced her hairline with his fingertips, his eyes moving over her face. He didn't look angry. Or even frustrated. If anything, his expression was sad.

"You don't feel like work to me. You're exactly what I want."

Veronica was beginning to believe him.

FOR THE SECOND MORNING IN A ROW, VERONICA WOKE UP in Jasper's arms. He was curled around her back, his knees pressed against the backs of her thighs. One arm acted as a pillow for her head and the other wrapped completely around her waist, his hand tucked between her body and the mattress.

He'd made love to her in the middle of the night, and she'd only had the energy to pull on her underwear before falling back into the bed. Though it was cool in the room, Jasper ran hotter than a normal human or even a typical supernatural. He put off enough heat to keep her toasty warm, even dressed in nothing but a skimpy pair of panties.

Veronica tried to slip from beneath his arm, but Jasper grunted and tightened his hold on her.

"Where you going?" he rumbled, his voice deep and rough from sleep.

"Bathroom."

With another grunt, he released her, and Veronica snagged his t-shirt off the floor, tugging it over her head as she headed into the bathroom. She washed her face and brushed her teeth while she was in there. When she came out, he was drinking a cup of coffee and holding another for her. The cabin came equipped with a single-cup coffee maker and pods, as well as sugar and tiny liquid creamer containers.

Grateful he'd made her coffee, Veronica took the cup and kissed his cheek. "Thank you."

"You're welcome. I ordered French toast, eggs, and bacon. The food should be delivered soon."

"Sounds delicious. Thanks." She sipped her coffee, humming in appreciation. He'd made it exactly as she liked it, with sugar and vanilla creamer.

"You don't have to thank me." He waited until she lowered her cup before he kissed her.

Veronica scrunched her nose at him when he pulled away and said, "I'll thank you if I want to and you'll take it."

Chuckling, Jasper sidled past her into the bathroom. "If you insist."

The food arrived before he came out, so Veronica accepted the brown paper bag and carried it into the kitchen. She liked that the food was delivered in containers rather than on porcelain plates or in glassware. It made it less likely that she would accidentally break something. She wasn't usually clumsy, but she always worried she would mess things up when she stayed at hotels or at someone's home.

The hotel must have spelled the containers to keep the food warm because it was still steaming when Jasper came into the kitchen and grabbed his plate. As they ate, Veronica asked him to go over the schedule for the day again.

"I'll have to head to the main lodge in a couple of hours. The groomsmen and Milo are all having lunch with my dad and Prema's dad. The ladies are doing the same thing with Mom and the bride's mother. After that, I'm sure we'll all be running herd on Milo to keep him away from Prema before the ceremony."

"When does the ceremony start again?" she asked.

"Four p.m. It will end at five and the guests will have a cocktail hour and hors d'oeuvres while the wedding party takes photos. The reception is supposed to start at six, but knowing my mother and Prema's mother, it will likely be six-fifteen or even six-thirty before we're done. They're going to want pictures of everything and everyone. Multiple pictures in case they don't like the first, second, or third options they get."

Veronica smiled. She hadn't spent much time with his parents, but if his mother was anything like him, she could see the woman wanting everything to be as perfect as possible.

"What are you going to do while I'm gone all day?" he asked.

She grinned. "I booked a mani-pedi in town. I'll probably have lunch while I'm there. Then, I think I'll read for a while before I get ready."

"I think I'd rather go with you," Jasper grumbled.

Veronica laughed and waved him off. "You should enjoy your day with your family. Your brother is only going to get married once."

"I hope so, because I'm not going through this rigamarole again."

"What about your own wedding?" she asked. "Surely your mother will insist on something like this for you."

Jasper shook his head. "Absolutely not. She already knows that I'm not having a three-ring circus when I get married. I've already informed her that I will probably elope. She threatened to disown me but changed her mind when I told her that was fine with me."

"She would never disown you."

"Probably not, but if it keeps me from having to do this when I get married, I'll happily accept it."

Shaking her head, Veronica took a sip of coffee.

"What about you? How do you envision your wedding day?" he asked.

She choked as her coffee went down the wrong way. Veronica bent over, coughing and sputtering, as she tried to clear her airway.

"Shit!" Jasper was kneeling beside her in a blink, gently patting her back. "Are you okay?"

She nodded, clearing her throat as the spasms began to subside. He jumped to his feet and came back a few moments later with a glass of water. Veronica gave him a grateful look as she took a sip.

It took a few more minutes of sipping water before she was able to speak again.

"I didn't realize asking you that question would bring on such a strong reaction," Jasper said. His tone was light, as though he were joking, but his eyes were serious on her.

"Honestly, I haven't thought much about it. I told you that I never thought I would get married. It's still not something I'm quite sure I could see for myself."

She left out the part that she could easily envision herself married to Jasper. They had only been together for a short time, but Veronica was falling hard and fast.

"Let's say you will get married someday. What do you see when you think about it?"

Veronica took a deep breath and let herself imagine that it could happen. That she would find someone who loved her, who she loved, and who she wanted to spend the rest of her life with. Her eyes drifted shut as she took a deep breath. In her head, she could see herself wearing a light, ethereal dress. Something like the mating gowns that fae women wore. She'd seen a picture of her great-grandmother's gown. It had flowed over her body like water, following the lines and curves of her figure. The material itself had been white but with an iridescent sheen. It looked like her great-grandmother had been wearing a prism beam. The colors were gentle and soft, but they changed with each angle and plane. Two thin straps held the dress up. Her shoulders were bare, but a drape of fabric hung from her bicep to her elbow, making graceful sleeves. The rest of the dress was utterly simple, following the contours of her great-grandmother's body to her knees before flaring out slightly to the floor.

Veronica could see herself wearing it, facing a man, and holding his hands. The sun was setting behind them and they were standing outside, surrounded by a very small group of people. If she was being completely honest, the man in her imagination had Jasper's face and some of the people around them were his parents and brother.

"What do you see?" he asked.

She opened her eyes. "I see myself standing outside at sunset, with only the man I'm marrying, our parents and siblings, and the officiant there. I'd wear my grandmother's fae mating gown and a crown of white flowers. There wouldn't be a reception, just a quiet dinner at our favorite restaurant. After that, my husband and I would go somewhere secluded, like a cabin in the forest or mountains, and we'd spend the next week with each other with no one else around."

She was smiling as she described it, able to see it so clearly that it almost felt as though she was there. When she focused on Jasper, he was studying her intently.

"That sounds perfect," he murmured.

The look on his face made her feel awkward and fidgety. She wanted to look away. The intense black gleam of his eyes felt like a brand on her skin. But she couldn't. Her eyes were locked on his, held in place by the force of his attention.

The spell was broken when his cell phone trilled from the bedroom, a loud, obnoxious melody echoing through the cabin.

Jasper blinked and sighed heavily. "I'm sure that's my mother with some sort of emergency. I changed her ringtone, but it never stays that way for long. I'll be back in a moment."

He left the dining table and disappeared into the bedroom. As soon as she heard him answer the phone, Veronica took a shaky breath. She wasn't sure what was happening in that moment, but it felt huge. Important.

As though the rest of her life were balanced on the edge of whatever Jasper might have said.

The murmur of Jasper's voice came from the bedroom. His tone was soothing, and Veronica knew he was probably talking to his mother. She smiled at the sound. As much as he pretended that she exasperated him, it was obvious that Jasper loved his mother. From her short interactions with both of them, she got the impression that they were very similar. They were both stubborn, used to getting their own way, and generous with the people they cared about. Veronica sensed that whoever Jasper chose to marry, the woman would be blessed beyond measure because he would do everything in his power to create a beautiful life with her.

She finished her breakfast and was drinking another cup of coffee when Jasper came out of the bedroom, his phone in his hand.

"Well, that was the first narrowly missed catastrophe of the day," he said.

She grinned. "What happened?"

"The florist got lost. Mom wanted me to go and get the woman and her employees, but I convinced her it was better to have one of the hotel staff help her find the way." He sighed and tossed his phone down on the table. "I'm going to shower before anything else happens. If the phone rings, throw it out the window. Or answer it and tell them I ran away."

Veronica laughed as he snagged his cup of cold coffee and vanished back into the bedroom.

CHAPTER FOURTEEN

VERONICA SMOOTHED her hand over her dress. The slinky material was a combination of deep blue and purple, the color shifting depending on the light. The halter neckline plunged to the base of her sternum, low enough to make her feel scandalous but narrow enough that she wasn't worried about a wardrobe malfunction. The skirt draped over her hips, gathered on each side. Despite the sexy style, the dress was surprisingly comfortable, which was the main reason she'd purchased it.

Her hair was styled in big, loose curls and she pinned it back on one side with a rhinestone clip in the shape of a crescent moon. When she went into town for her manicure and pedicure, the nail tech, Brenna, asked her what she was doing in Devil Springs. Veronica explained that she was staying at the Devil's Playground for a wedding. They chatted for a while and Brenna asked her what she was wearing. The discussion moved from there to hair and make-up and Veronica admitted that she had no idea what she was going to do with her make-up. She explained that she usually kept her style simple and always went for understated looks to most of the formal events she attended for work. Now that she had the opportunity to wear something bolder, she had no idea what to do.

Her admission made Brenna smile broadly and say, "Oh, hon. I know just the person to help you out."

Brenna made a call, and fifteen minutes later, a woman walked into the shop that made Veronica look twice. She wasn't very tall, but she carried herself with a posture that made her seem taller. Veronica wanted to tell Brenna not to bother when she got a look at the woman's outfit and hairstyle. She wore all black, her t-shirt torn and ripped in a way that was designed to show skin and look sexy. Her black jeans were faded and skintight, tucked into knee-high combat boots. Even her hair was black. The mass was cut in tons of layers and surrounded her face in messy, chunky waves.

It wasn't until she was closer that Veronica saw her face and realized why Brenna called her. The woman's make-up was gorgeous. Heavy enough to be noticeable, but not overly done. She looked like a model.

"Veronica Salt, this is Lilith Brightstar," Brenna said.

Lilith's smile was small as she shook Veronica's hand. Her mental shields were locked down so tight that Veronica couldn't feel any emotion coming from her.

"You told Brenna you were going to a wedding, yes?" Lilith asked. When Veronica nodded, she continued, "Do you have a picture of the dress?"

The saleswoman at the store had insisted on taking pictures of Veronica in her final three selections so she could decide which she preferred, claiming it would give her a realistic idea of how the dress looked. Veronica found the image on her phone and showed it to Lilith.

The woman's smile grew a bit wicked. "Very sexy. And the color is a good choice for you. Do you mind if we keep this on the screen so I can look back at it while we're doing your face?"

Once Veronica agreed, Brenna settled her on a tall stool next to the counter that ran along one side of the store. One end held a single-cup coffee maker with an assortment of pods and paper cups and the other held hair and beauty products the salon sold to their clients. The middle was clear and obviously used for seating.

Lilith went outside and quickly returned with a matte black train case. When she opened it up on the counter, Veronica's eyes bugged out, drawing a genuine laugh from the woman.

"I like to play with make-up," she said. "I find it relaxing."

Lilith didn't talk much as she brushed, smoothed, dabbed, and blended different products on Veronica's face, but it was restful. Even relaxing. Though it was much longer than she ever spent on her own make-up, Veronica was still surprised by how quickly Lilith seemed to get it done.

It couldn't have been more than twenty or thirty minutes when the woman stepped back and said, "All done."

Brenna had just started a manicure on a woman, but she looked over and her mouth dropped open in awe. "Veronica, you look amazing!"

"Go take a look," Lilith invited.

Veronica went to the mirror and nearly gaped at the woman staring back at her. It was her, but it was as if Lilith had played up her best features and diminished her weakest. She felt a little like the Photo-chopped version of herself.

When she returned to the counter, Veronica thanked Lilith profusely. The woman accepted her compliments with the same small smile she wore when they were introduced, but her demeanor was quiet and aloof.

Veronica tried to pay her for the service, but she waved it off. "This is fun for me. As I said, it's how I relax. Enjoy the wedding and the rest of your stay in Devil Springs."

Fast forward to now, Veronica was fully dressed, her hair done, her make-up touched up, and she was standing in the hallway that led into the ballroom where the ceremony was being held. Her heart was pounding in her chest because she was about to enter a room crammed full of people and she could already feel their emotions nudging and shoving her. Most of them were positive, which made it easier to deal with, but there were a few people whose bitterness, jealousy, and annoyance scrapped against her mental shields.

Veronica shut her eyes and took a deep breath, holding it for a long moment before she released it. As she did, she focused on rebuilding the walls around her mind. She'd been so relaxed with Jasper and Lilith that this sudden onslaught was almost overwhelming.

Gradually, the emotional "noise" faded away and her shoulders relaxed. When she opened her eyes, the first thing she saw was Jasper standing a few feet away, his eyes glued to her.

The expression on his face was the same one he wore when he'd made love to her the night before—intense, bold, and hot. Just as it had last night, his gaze made goosebumps break out on her body, racing down her arms and legs. Thankfully, the dress had built-in bra cups to hide the fact that her nipples were suddenly hard.

Unsmiling, Jasper moved toward her, practically shouldering his way past his family members when they tried to stop and talk to him. Everyone seemed to take his rudeness in stride, which told Veronica that he likely behaved like this a lot.

He didn't stop until he was less than a foot away and Veronica could feel the heat pouring off his body. She tilted her chin up to keep her eyes on his, but his stare moved all over her face.

"You look beautiful," he murmured. His hand curled around hers, tugging her closer until they were nearly touching. "I almost didn't recognize you."

She smiled even as she blushed. "Thank you. There was a woman at the salon who did my make-up after my appointment."

"Make-up? I didn't even notice. I was looking at your dress." The tip of one finger trailed from the center of her collarbones down to the bottom of the plunging neckline, tracing over the narrow sliver of skin it bared.

Veronica grabbed his hand before he could hook his finger into the material that gathered at the base of her sternum. "Behave," she murmured.

"Only because we don't have any privacy," he sighed, taking a small step back, but retaining his grip on her hand. "Let's get you seated before one of my lady-killer cousins decide they want to try to lure you away from me."

"Lure? Like a fish?"

Sensing the offense in her tone, Jasper smirked at her. "I'm sure you couldn't be lured, but I'd have to kill the little bastards, which would upset my brother, my sister-in-law, and my parents. So, let's avoid bloodshed and get you settled."

Veronica rolled her eyes as he guided her down the aisle, stopping just behind the front row of chairs and gesturing to the second row.

"Jasper, I can't sit here. It's reserved for family," she argued.

"You're here with me and I'm related to the groom, so this is exactly where you belong."

Before she could continue arguing, Jasper's father came up behind them. "Hello, Veronica. You look stunning." After she thanked him, he turned to his son. "Jas, it's almost time. The ceremony is starting in five minutes and the wedding planner is about to begin foaming at the mouth because we're already thirty seconds behind schedule."

"She's timed it down to the second?" Jasper asked, incredulous. At his father's dry look, he leaned over and kissed Veronica lightly on the mouth. "Stay here so I can see you during the ceremony. After I escape the picture-taking portion of the evening, I'll hunt you down at the reception."

There was nothing else she could do but agree. "All right."

"Good girl." He kissed her one more time before he followed his father toward the back of the room. She should have been offended by his words, but they gave her a secret thrill. Before she decided how she felt, he followed his father toward the back of the room.

Veronica couldn't resist turning around to watch him. He looked gorgeous in his tux. As though he belonged on the cover of one of the billionaire romance novels she read. When he vanished from view, her eyes skimmed over the crowd, coming to rest on Prema's younger sister, Jasmine. Standing in the open double doors that Veronica had just come through, the woman watched her with a distasteful expression on her face. Veronica could practically feel the jealousy and anger buzzing around her from across the ballroom. The emotions felt like tiny daggers embedding themselves into her skin.

The string ensemble near the wedding arch began to play and Veronica turned around. It was clear that Jasmine had an issue with her, but she couldn't address it unless the other woman approached her about it. Honestly, she hoped the woman gave her a wide berth. She had enough mental upheaval and confusion already.

As everyone took their seats and the officiant took her place beneath the wedding arch, Veronica pushed thoughts of Jasmine out of her mind. It wasn't easy to do, but she'd learned over the years to accept that other people were responsible for their own feelings. If someone seemed aloof or rude or angry, she shouldn't take it to heart because those emotions and reactions might not be instigated by her actions.

The ceremony was lovely. Veronica especially enjoyed the gorgeous dress that Prema wore. The sweetheart neckline and slightly off-the-shoulder sleeves were a blush so pale it was nearly pure white. But the bodice became a darker pink, the color bleeding across the fabric as though it was watercolor paint on paper. Then, from the cinched waist to the big bell skirt, the color grew darker until it was a brilliant blood red on the lower part of the gown. The ombre effect was set on a diagonal, as though the dress had been dipped into the dye after it was made. Though the structure and design of the gown was traditional and reminded Veronica of something a princess would wear, the change of color in the material elevated it to something akin to artwork.

She couldn't help tearing up as Milo and Prema exchanged their vows. They were so sweet and heartfelt that Veronica couldn't suppress the flash of jealousy that pierced her heart. It quickly faded, but she couldn't get the pictures she'd conjured up in her imagination this morning off her mind. The mental image of her in her great-grandmother's wedding dress, looking up at Jasper as she said her wedding vows. In her head, she looked at him the way Prema was looking at Milo, as though he was the center of her universe.

The ceremony ended and the bridal party walked back down the aisle. She noticed the way that Jasmine clung to Jasper's arm, resting her weight against him. She also saw the triumphant look the woman shot her as they walked by during the recessional. Veronica suppressed a sigh because it was clear she was going to have to endure the other woman's nastiness for the rest of the evening.

Once the wedding party was out of the room, people began to leave their seats and migrate out the doors. The cocktail hour was in the small bar area in the lobby, people spilling out into the lobby when there wasn't enough room. Veronica floated around the edges of the crowd, nodding at people she'd seen before.

Eventually, she worked her way to the bar and accepted a glass of white wine. Between the noise of people chattering at each other and the emotions zipping around the room, Veronica was beginning to feel a bit overwhelmed. She found a small alcove down a wide hallway at the rear of the lobby. The counter appeared to be a spot to rest laptops or notebooks, but Veronica hopped up on top of it and leaned back against the wall. She drank her wine and tried to relax. She'd enjoyed talking to Jasper's family members and his sister-in-law's family, though she'd had yet to meet his infamous Aunt Samira and her daughter, Mina.

She closed her eyes, letting her head rest against the wall behind her. As she began to relax, two female voices filtered into the alcove from the hallway.

"I wasn't sure about this place when we got here. The exterior and cabins are so...rustic. But they did a beautiful job on transforming the ballroom."

"They did."

"It's a shame that Jasper brought a date this weekend. I thought for sure he would end up with Jasmine. Can you imagine? Two brothers marrying two sisters. It's so romantic."

Veronica's eyes popped open, and she lifted her head when she heard Jasper's name. She set her wineglass to the side as she leaned forward and continued to listen. It might be rude to eavesdrop, but she had a feeling this conversation might open her eyes to whatever was making the bride's younger sister so resentful of her.

"Darya tried to arrange it. Jasmine developed a crush on Jasper as soon as the families were introduced. Her mother likes him as well, so they were both doing everything they could to finesse the situation."

The other woman made a humming sound. "Have you met the woman Jasper brought this weekend?"

"No, Mina, I haven't. She's very pretty and seems quite taken with him, but your Aunt Leila told me that the girl is an empath." The voice tutted. "I don't see how she would be a good fit for Jasper or this family. Nothing against empaths, but they don't handle noise or conflict well and that's something we have in spades. Jasper would have to change himself completely just to make her happy. I don't see it lasting once the initial attraction fades."

Veronica's stomach clenched. She had a sinking feeling that she was listening to Jasper's aunt, Samira, talking to her daughter, Mina. And how did his mother know she was an empath? When did he tell his parents?

"I don't think I agree, Mama. I've never seen Jasper look at anyone the way he looks at her, not even Melina and we all thought they would get engaged."

"I just can't believe that your aunt Leila isn't pitching a fit about this. She's always thought she would have to pick his wife for him."

Veronica's eyes widened. Jasper's mom thought she was going to pick his wife for him?

"Leila seems to like her a lot," Mina replied. "So does Cyrus. Milo said he's been waiting a long time for Jasper to meet someone like her. And that he hopes she gives Jasper hell."

Samira chuckled. "Your Cousin Milo is a character." She fell silent for a moment. When she spoke again, her voice was quieter and deeper, as though she didn't want to be overheard. "I just don't think she's a good fit for him or this family. Especially given how they met."

"How did they meet?" Mina asked.

"Well, according to Leila and Cyrus, Jasper joined a matchmaking service to find a date for this weekend. And the girl works there. Personally, I can't believe she would do something so unprofessional. I mean, really...to date a client. That seems wrong."

Veronica's chest ached when she heard those words. Was that what his family thought of her? That she was unprofessional because she was dating him? His mother was a businesswoman. Professionalism and ethics would be incredibly important to her.

The women stopped talking when a voice called out Samira's name. Veronica sat on the counter for a long time after they moved away, her stomach twisting viciously as their words echoed in her mind.

Finally, she heard the crowd filtering away and realized the reception was about to start. Her legs were shaky as she slid off the counter. She held onto it until she felt steadier. Though she no longer wanted it, Veronica finished off her glass of wine. She was going to need it to get through the evening.

As she emerged from the alcove and headed toward the lobby, empty wineglass in hand, she stopped short when Jasmine appeared in front of her. The animosity rolled off the younger woman in waves as her gaze moved over Veronica, taking in her shoes, dress, make-up, and hair. By the sneer on her face, she found all of it lacking.

"Hello," Veronica murmured.

"You shouldn't be here," Jasmine stated, her words low. "You don't belong here."

Still shaken from what she'd overheard Samira and Mina say, Veronica just stared at the young woman in silence. Jasmine seemed to take that as an invitation to continue.

"Jasper is supposed to be my date. My mother arranged it with his. I showed up alone this weekend, like a loser, because it was all decided."

Though her mouth was dry, Veronica managed to speak. "I'm sure it was just a misunderstanding. I should—"

Her words died in her throat when Jasmine stepped closer, her anger intensifying. Veronica leaned back, trying to keep space between them because the weight of the woman's anger and other emotions.

"You're not good enough for Jasper," Jasmine sneered.

Though she wanted to run away and hide to avoid the nasty emotions slicing her, Veronica managed to straighten her back and square her shoulders. "I believe it's Jasper's decision about who he spends his time with and who is good enough for him. But in reality, there is no *good enough* or *worthy enough*. Either he loves me the way I am, just as I love him the way he is, or he doesn't. I don't have to qualify for that emotion from him. He either loves me or he doesn't. I don't have to earn it." As she said the words, Veronica realized they were true. All these years, she felt unlovable and unworthy, but it wasn't the case.

A hard arm wrapped around her waist before she could say anything else, pulling her back into a tall, strong body. Jasper held her so close that she could barely breathe.

"Good evening, Jasmine. While I was aware that my mother and yours were trying to pair us up for this weekend, it was never going to happen. Veronica is right. I decide who I want to spend time with. Not Darya. Not my own mother. Me. No matter what they scheme or plan, I will choose my own path." He paused, moving Veronica to his side and pulling her into him. "As for Veronica belonging here, I think you should resign yourself to seeing her at our combined family functions for a very long time. Probably the rest of my life."

Jasper didn't wait for Jasmine to reply. He practically carried Veronica away from her, heading in the opposite direction of the reception, which was taking place in the same ballroom where the ceremony had been performed.

His steps didn't slow until he found a bathroom and shoved the door open. It was a large family restroom, so he hauled her inside, shut the door behind them, and locked it. All the while, hugging her to his side.

Once the door was locked, though, he released her and planted his back against it, clearly intent on blocking her only means of exit.

His black eyes were burning with dark fire as he looked down at her. Veronica wanted step back, but she couldn't move.

She was trapped.

CHAPTER FIFTEEN

JASPER HAD HEARD everything she said. Everything.

And it was taking every bit of his willpower to keep his hands off her.

"You love me?" he asked.

She took a step back, which he didn't like. Not at all. Jasper took a step forward, keeping the distance between them the same.

"Do you?" he pushed.

Veronica's face turned bright red, the blush working its way down her neck and into her chest. "Jasper…"

When she didn't finish her thought, he took another step forward. She backed up and kept backing up until her back was pressed against the opposite wall.

"Why won't you answer me?" he asked.

Her eyes darted everywhere but his face. He hooked a finger beneath her chin, tilting it up. "Look at me."

Blinking rapidly, she did as he demanded.

"My father always told me that I would know the woman who was meant for me when I saw her. He said that within ten minutes of meeting her, he knew my mother was the woman for him. That he would love her for the rest of his life. I have him beat because I knew the moment you looked up at me from behind your computer at Mystical Matchmakers. It was like a kick to the gut, but it didn't hurt at all."

Her eyes grew shiny at his words. "Don't you think it's too soon?"

"Ten minutes, remember? I've known you for six weeks. Almost seven. That seems like a lifetime in comparison. Just tell me how you feel, Veronica."

She took a shaky breath, her eyes still damp. "I'm falling for you. When I told you about my vision of my own wedding, it was your face I saw."

He cupped her face, kissing her lightly. "I was ready to cancel my membership last week. Not because I still didn't want a date, but because I was hoping you'd finally say yes when I asked you out if I was no longer a client."

"It's crazy. We barely know each other."

"It's not crazy to me. Things are happening exactly like they're supposed to."

He kissed her again, deeper and harder this time. His hands went around her waist, pulling her closer. Veronica leaned into him, her hands clutching at his shoulders and back, fingertips digging into his muscles.

When he cupped her ass and lifted her, she moaned against his tongue and twined her legs around his hips. There was a small chaise lounge against the wall to his left. Jasper carried her over there and sat down with her on his lap.

Some of Veronica's shyness had vanished the night before and even more seemed to be gone tonight. She rocked against him, her fingers fisting his hair and the heat of her pussy pressing against his cock.

His fingers slipped beneath the bottom hem of her dress, pushing the fabric above her hips, baring the tiny, sheer panties she wore. He cupped and rubbed her hips before latching one hand on each globe of her ass. He controlled her movements, rocking her slower and harder.

Her fingers twisted in his hair, making his scalp sting, but Jasper loved it. It meant that Veronica was losing herself in the moment, just like he was.

He released her ass and ran a hand up her bare back to the halter strap that secured the dress behind her neck. With a quick tug, the knot was undone, and the material fell away from her breasts.

She wasn't wearing a bra beneath the garment and her nipples were flushed and peaked as he looked at them and ran the tip of his tongue over them. Veronica reached down and started slipping the buttons free from his shirt. She shoved the fabric apart and leaned down to run her tongue and lips over his chest and neck. He lifted her off his lap, setting her on her feet in front of him.

Reaching beneath the skirt of her dress, he hooked the straps of her panties with his fingers and pulled them down. Once she was bare, he leaned back and tackled his own belt and pants. As soon as he pulled his cock free, Veronica dropped to her knees in front of him, her eyes locked on his erection.

He hissed out a breath when she leaned forward and opened her mouth. He couldn't speak as her tongue stroked up one side of his dick before flicking the head. Bit by bit, she slid more of him into her mouth, sucking, licking, and using her hand to stroke him. Jasper's head fell back, and he groaned as she took him deeper. Careful not to hurt her, he fisted his hands in her hair. He didn't push or shove her head, just held on for dear life because her mouth felt amazing.

As he got close to the edge, he tightened his hold on her curls. "Hold on, Veronica. Wait."

She didn't hear him because she kept going, sucking even harder and nearly making him come in her mouth.

"Stop, Veronica," he demanded.

She lifted her mouth off his cock, her lips shiny, and swallowed. "Why?"

His answer was to yank her up onto his lap and settle her on top of him. His hands explored her breasts and ass before his right hand moved to her pussy. He groaned again when his index finger trailed over her clit to her slippery entrance.

"Sucking my dick turned you on, didn't it?" he asked.

She nodded instead of answering out loud, something she still did with him sometimes. Part of it was her innate shyness and the rest was that she was so consumed by the sensations he evoked in her body that she couldn't speak, much less think clearly enough to form a complete sentence.

Gathering the wetness from her pussy, he brought it to her clit and circled the little nub. Veronica's hips moved in time with his touch, pressing down harder into his hand.

"You're ready for me, aren't you?"

"Yes," she whispered, her body moving to ride his hand harder and faster.

Her breath caught in her throat as her muscles spasmed around his fingers. Jasper held her still, keeping his hand exactly where it was as she hovered on the edge of orgasm. The need to come was so strong it hurt, and Veronica released a soft whimper as she fought the urge to move.

Jasper pulled his hand free, grasped her hips, and positioned her over his lap. She reached down and grabbed his dick, moving it exactly where she needed it. Using his grip on her hips, he urged her lower. Veronica's head fell back as she sank down on him, his cock sliding in deep due to how wet she was.

Her pussy clenched around him as her orgasm threatened to break free. Jasper held her down, keeping himself fully embedded in her body as he guided her hips back and forth, rocking her against him.

"Are you gonna come for me?" he asked, slipping one hand over the crease where her hip met her thigh. His thumb rested over her clit, not moving as she continued rocking against him. When she didn't answer, he pinched it lightly, tugging her clit with slow, firm pressure. "Answer me, Veronica."

"Yes," she whispered.

The pressure of his fingers on her clit made it pulse in time with her movements. Then, he released it, pressed his thumb firmly against it, and rubbed. Within a minute, Veronica's body bowed, and her legs shook. Jasper increased the speed and intensity of the caress until she stopped moving, trembling all over. With her body positioned on his lap, Jasper took advantage of the position and leaned forward to pull one of her nipples into his mouth, suckling it gently.

Veronica broke with a cry, but he released her hip long enough to grab her hair and tilt her head down so he could kiss her, swallowing down the noises she made as she came all over his cock. Moments later, he stiffened beneath her, his body drawing tight from the force of his own orgasm.

They were both breathing heavy when he finally released her mouth. Veronica rested her forehead against his, shivering on his lap. As their bodies cooled, the sounds of people walking down the hall and talking filtered through the door. No one had tried to enter the bathroom yet, but it was only a matter of time before someone tried to open the door.

Jasper didn't much give a damn if his family realized he'd fucked his date in the bathroom, but he knew Veronica would be embarrassed. She wanted to make a good impression with his family.

Slowly, he pulled back, brushing her hair away from her face. "You know what Jasmine said is bullshit, right? You do belong here with me. With my family. There isn't anyone who could be better for me than you."

Her expression became guarded, and it caused a twisting sensation in his chest. "About that..." She looked down. "Let me get cleaned up and then we'll talk."

He wanted to argue, but he could feel his cum slipping out of her and he didn't want to get it all over his pants. He spied a box of tissues on a table beside the chaise. Jasper grabbed the entire box, pulling a handful of tissues out.

It took a little maneuvering, but he caught most of the mess with the tissues as she climbed off him. Veronica moved to the sink, her dress still rucked up around her hips. She wet a paper towel and cleaned between her legs before she started looking around for her underwear. Jasper saw them on the couch next to his hip. He was tempted to stick them in his pocket, but, again, he knew it would make her uncomfortable to walk around bare beneath her dress with his family around.

Maybe he could work her up to that in the future.

Smirking at the thought, Jasper picked up the filmy thong, letting it dangle from his index finger by the strap on the side. "Looking for these?"

Seeing his smirk, Veronica sighed and walked over to take them. "What's got that look on your face?" she asked.

"I was just wondering how long we'll have to be together before you let me carry your panties in my pocket after we sneak off to mess around at my family gatherings."

She sat next to him, threading the panties over her heeled sandals before standing up to tug them up her legs. He watched in interest as she did a little shimmy to pull the straps over her hips. Her ass had four red dots on the cheek, and he realized his fingertips had left the marks.

"Do these hurt?" he asked, running a finger over them.

Veronica looked down over her shoulder, but she couldn't see what he was touching. "What is it?"

"You have red marks on you from my fingers. Do they hurt?"

She shook her head.

"Will they bruise?" he asked.

"Probably not."

Jasper tried to pretend he wasn't a little disappointed, but she saw right through it and smiled a little. "Sorry, Jas. I don't bruise easily."

His eyes lifted to hers when she used his nickname. Then, he smiled. "I like it when you call me that."

"Jas?"

He nodded, watching as she shimmied again, this time to tug her dress down over her hips and settle it in place. Jasper couldn't resist running his hand up the back of her leg, marveling at the softness of her skin.

Veronica shivered and sidestepped his touch. "Jasper," she said, his name a clear reprimand.

"What?" he asked as he stood.

"We need to get to the reception. Your family already thinks poorly of me and—"

"Whoa. Back up. My family thinks *poorly of you*? Who told you that?" Whoever it was would regret their words.

Veronica sighed. "This is what I wanted to talk to you about." She bit her lip. "God, I really need another glass of wine before we talk about this, but I think it's better if we have privacy when we do."

His heart gave a quick double thump before it sank in his chest. She looked sad and upset. He didn't care who it was who put that look on her face, but he would make it very clear that it would never happen again. Even if it was his own mother.

She took a deep breath and released it before she continued, "I was resting in the alcove in the hallway after the ceremony, just getting a little break from the cocktail party. Your aunt, Samira, and her daughter were chatting right outside. They didn't know I was in there."

Jasper scowled. "What did they say?"

"Nothing really bad," Veronica assured him. "But your aunt seemed concerned that I worked for the matchmaker service. She thought it was unprofessional for me to date a client and said she was surprised your mother didn't think so, too."

Jasper tried not to react, but she was observant enough to see the subtle change in his expression.

"Did she say something like that?" Veronica asked.

"Yes, but it was because she didn't understand what really happened. Just like Samira doesn't understand. If she did, she would know that dating a client was the last thing you wanted to do."

"She's not wrong," Veronica pointed out.

"I don't care what she thinks," Jasper stated. "And I don't want you to care either. The only thing that matters to me is that you're happy and that I'm happy. Aunt Samira, Mina, even my mother, don't affect what happens between you and me."

Veronica's smile was tremulous. "Well, Samira also seemed concerned that I was an empath. That I would want to keep you away from your family because being around them would overwhelm me." She cleared her throat. "She said your mother told her, so I'm guessing you told your parents?"

She took a tiny step back when she saw the look on his face.

"I did tell my parents. And my brother. I'm sorry that I didn't share that with you. I wanted to let you be the one to tell them, but I also wanted them to understand that you were going to be my priority this weekend and why."

He still looked enraged. Veronica shifted back another step.

"I understand, Jasper," she whispered. "I'm not upset about that. Your parents and Milo had a right to know about what I am. This is supposed to be a happy family event and, well—"

"Don't say anything negative about yourself," he commanded. "You are exactly who you should be."

Veronica pressed her lips together and swallowed hard. God, she had no idea how to respond when he said things like that.

After a few tense moments, Jasper sighed and slumped forward.

"This was one hell of a conversation for you to overhear while you were trying to relax in peace," he muttered, a fierce scowl taking over his face. His black eyes glittered with fury. "It was also one hell of a conversation for them to be having at what should be the happy family event you mentioned."

Oh, no. This was not what Veronica wanted. She hadn't wanted to talk about it now because she didn't want to cause drama at his brother's wedding. She wasn't as doubtful about Jasper's motivations or feelings toward her as she had been earlier, so the conversation no longer seemed like a big issue to her. She crossed the room until she stood in front of him.

Putting a hand on his arm, she said, "Jasper, please don't get upset and confront your aunt. Nothing she said seemed to come from maliciousness. The only impression I got off her was that she was concerned about you and that she was sincerely worried our relationship might not be good for you."

Jasper stepped into her, lowering his head as he used both hands to cradle the back of her head beneath her fall of hair. "I am a grown man, Veronica. While I appreciate that my aunt loves me, she doesn't need to concern herself with my romantic decisions unless I ask for her opinion."

Veronica bit her bottom lip as she stared up at him. "Her heart was in the right place, Jas," she said, putting her hands on his chest.

"Please don't make a scene today. It's about Milo and Prema. Not about you and your aunt."

Knowing she was right, Jasper sighed. "Fine. I won't say anything today, but my aunt and I *will* be having a talk tomorrow or Monday. And I will make it clear that any thoughts she has about you and my relationship should stay in her brain and not come out of her mouth. Or, if she absolutely has to say something, she should talk to me or her daughter in private and not at a crowded event where anyone, especially the woman I care about, can overhear her." He leaned down and dropped a kiss on her lips. "And don't think I didn't notice how you used my nickname to soften me up."

"Did it work?" she asked.

His only answer was to kiss her again.

CHAPTER SIXTEEN

THE PARTY WAS in full swing when they entered the ballroom. Two lines snaked down the row of tables in the back, one on each side, and people were filling plates of food. Those who had already gotten their food were seated at the large round tables that had been set up during the cocktail hour.

Though his mother had wanted an actual dinner service for the wedding, the resort hadn't been able to accommodate that much staff or food preparation, so she and Prema's mother had agreed that a buffet-style dinner would work best.

Jasper was relieved because it meant that he didn't have to choose a single meal but was able to try a little bit of everything. There was even a dessert buffet and an open bar.

He craned his head, looking around the room for his aunt. Though he wasn't going to confront her tonight, he wanted to let her know that they needed to talk. Preferably soon.

Instead of finding Samira and Mina, his gaze landed on Jasmine Shah and the glare she was shooting toward him. No, toward Veronica. His eyes narrowed and, as though she could sense his attention, Jasmine's glare shifted to him. When their stares clashed, she blinked and looked away almost immediately. For whatever reason, her anger that he wasn't going to fall in line was directed solely at Veronica and Jasper did not like that.

He wasn't going to concern himself with it unless she continued to make it a problem. And, as Veronica said, tonight was not the night to address the issue.

Jasper's gaze swept the rest of the ballroom before coming to a stop on his brother, who was standing shoulder-to-shoulder with his dad. Both men were looking right at him, their arms crossed over their chests and smug grins on their faces. His brother looked down and tapped his watch before wiggling his eyebrows at Jasper.

Knowing his brother was subtly giving him shit for disappearing with his date and screwing around in the bathroom, Jasper pretended to scratch one of his eyebrows with his middle finger.

From across the room, he could see his father sigh at his reaction, but the smug grin returned quickly. His dad was happy for him for a different reason—he was glad that Jasper had finally found the woman he wanted for the rest of his life.

He was grateful he'd had trouble finding a date for the wedding this weekend and his mother threatened to set him up with Jasmine. If she hadn't, he would never have called Mystical Matchmakers.

Jasper slipped an arm around Veronica's waist when she stepped away to allow one of his many cousins pass between them. A male cousin who was eyeing her like she was a tasty little snack.

"Chad," Jasper said in greeting.

His cousin shot him a glare. "Stop calling me that." He turned on the charm as he faced Veronica. "My name is Casper. I'm Jasper's younger, better-looking cousin."

Veronica nodded at him but didn't offer her hand to shake, which pleased him. "Nice to meet you, Casper." She glanced at Jasper. "Why do you call him Chad?"

"Because Casper and Jasper rhyme and, since I'm older, I get to keep my name. He has to be Chad."

Jasper saw the quirk of her lips and the brief hint of the small dimple that sometimes appeared in her cheek when she laughed particularly hard.

"I see."

"So, how did you guys meet?" Casper asked Veronica.

"Bye, Chad," Jasper replied, using his hold on Veronica's waist to steer her away.

"Stop calling me that!"

He felt her shoulders shaking as they walked and knew she was trying not to laugh while his cousin was in earshot.

When they were far enough away, he said, "Don't hurt yourself. He can't hear you anymore."

Veronica gave a small snort. It was the cutest sound he'd ever heard. He loved her laugh, but that snort was on another level. She released a quiet giggle and swatted him on the belly.

"Why were you so mean to him?" she murmured.

"Because he was going to flirt with you right in front of me and now, he knows that's unacceptable."

She nodded. "He obviously likes to irritate you. I could sense his pleasure at irking you."

Jasper shrugged. "We grew up around each other, so we act more like siblings than cousins."

"Well, he loves you, if that helps."

He sighed. "I know. It's my cross to bear. I'm so lovable."

Veronica started laughing again and said, "I'm almost sad for the wedding to be over and go home tomorrow. Your family is pretty entertaining."

Jasper guided her toward the buffet lines, his mind stuck on what she said about the wedding being over. He hadn't let himself consider it, but tomorrow, they would be leaving after the brunch and going back to Dallas. He would have to take Veronica to her apartment...and go home alone.

He hated the idea. They had only been here for two and a half days, but he'd gotten used to waking up with her and going to sleep with her. And even though they spent the last two days apart, he'd looked forward to going back to their cabin and finding her there. He didn't want to go home to an empty house tomorrow.

He wanted her to stay with him every day. He wanted to learn about her habits, even if some of them might drive him crazy. He wanted to truly know her, though he doubted he would ever get to the point where there was no mystery to her. Veronica felt things too deeply and spent a lot of time in her own head. She was a difficult woman to learn, and it would likely take him decades to do it.

He looked forward to it.

Jasper also knew that she wouldn't want to move in with him so soon. He knew what he wanted, and he was ready to make the move, but Veronica still had to catch up. Yes, she said she was falling for him, but she expressed her worries that it was too soon for that conversation. If he brought up the idea of her moving in with him, or vice versa, because he honestly didn't give a shit where they lived, she would balk.

Still, he would figure out how to get what he wanted. He always did. This time he knew it would require compromise, but as long as he got time with her, he didn't care.

He managed to be polite to his family when they interrupted what he considered his last full day with Veronica. He also found time to track down his aunt and let Samira know that they would be having a conversation on Monday after work. Judging by the look on her face, she knew why he was upset.

Surprisingly, she just nodded and said she would call him after dinner on Monday.

The only reason Jasper didn't hurry Veronica out of the reception after they ate, and his brother and Prema cut the cake, was because the band his mother hired started playing and the music was good. Perfect for holding her close and swaying.

He may not be an empath, but he'd noticed how much she seemed to crave touch. Not just sexual, but affectionate and casual touch as well. If he put his arm around her, she leaned into him. If he scooted his chair closer to hers, she angled her body, so her thigh pressed against his. If he took her hand, she would lace their fingers together.

The biggest giveaway was the way she behaved in her sleep. When she slept next to him, she plastered her body against his in her slumber. If he got up, she would roll away, only to turn over and wrap herself around him like a vine when he returned to the bed. It was as if she was seeking maximum contact when she was fully relaxed, and her guards were down.

He didn't tell her because he knew she would be embarrassed. And if she felt embarrassed, she might try to stop. Jasper didn't want that. He liked having her right next to him all night, even if his arm went numb from her head lying on his bicep. Or his hip ached from digging into the mattress when she all but draped her weight over his back when he was on his stomach.

Still, after an hour of dancing, he was ready to leave and have her to himself. They said their good-byes and went back to the cabin, where he "helped" her take off her dress. Which meant they ended up naked in the bed, where he made love to her again. Then, he spent the night pinned to the bed by her weight, something he enjoyed immensely.

He did the same the next morning, only this time, he made her come twice with his mouth before he pulled her on top of him and had her ride him again. It was a view he could get used to.

The brunch wasn't as loud or crazy as the wedding, probably because most of his relatives and family friends were hungover from their indulgences the night before. His mother made an effort to chat with Veronica, making it clear to him that she liked her. He knew it was mostly because she wanted him to know that she approved, but the added benefit was that Jasmine had a front row seat to the maternal approval Leila was bestowing on Veronica.

He didn't need to be an empath like his woman to understand that Prema's younger sister was bitter with jealousy.

Resolutely, he ignored it. Giving her any sort of attention would only feed her need for drama. As long as she didn't do or say anything to upset Veronica, he wasn't going to entertain her attitude.

They finished the brunch, gave his parents, brother, and new sister-in-law hugs, and returned to their cabin to pack. Veronica seemed distant. Lost in her own thoughts.

Jasper gave her space and a chance to figure out whatever was in her head, but when she still hadn't talked to him about it when they were packing up the car, he decided to address the issue head-on.

He took her hand when she turned to walk from the rear of his car to the passenger door, stopping her. "Is something bothering you, Veronica?" he asked.

She huffed out a laugh. "Yes. I'm sorry. I'm not upset with you or anything. Just stuck in my head."

He lifted his free hand and stroked his thumb over her cheek. "Tell me."

Her answering smile was a little sad. "I feel kind of silly."

"I don't care if it's silly. I want to understand what's bothering you so I can help if I'm able."

Her eyes were soft as she returned his stare and, to his surprise, she didn't dance around the answer. "It's only been three days, but I've gotten used to having you around. I'm not ready for you to go yet."

He used his hold on her hand to pull her closer and smiled. "That's good because I feel the same way."

She shocked the shit out of him yet again. Sly Veronica licked her lips and asked, "Would you come home with me today? And stay tonight?"

"I was hoping you'd come home with me."

He could immediately tell she didn't like that idea. "My house is comfortable and fully stocked. I think you'll love it," he explained.

She relaxed a little. "I'm sure I will. It's just…" She paused and he could tell she was choosing her words carefully.

"You don't have to worry about hurting my feelings. I'd rather you be honest about what you're thinking and feeling."

"It's not that," she replied. "I'm just not sure how to describe it in a way that won't come across as entitled and that you'll understand."

"How about you say whatever it is you're thinking, and I'll understand that you're not trying to be entitled, but just telling me how you feel?"

"Okay." She took a deep breath. "Changes in environment are difficult for me. Especially coming off a weekend like this one where I've been around a lot of people. I'll recover faster at my own apartment with my own things around me. And I'll be able to relax more."

"I completely understand that. How about I drop you at your apartment, go home to get some clothes, and come back to stay with you for a couple of nights. Once you're feeling back to normal, we'll spend some time at my place."

Her hands tightened around his. "Are you sure you're okay with that?"

"Will I get to see you this week if I do what I just described?"

She nodded, looking confused.

"Then, of course I'm okay with that."

Her hands tightened on his and she blurted out, "I'm so sorry I didn't say yes the first or second time you asked me out. I really wish I had."

Jasper pulled her into his arms, and she wrapped hers so tightly around his waist that he had a little trouble breathing. She took a shaky breath, as though she was fighting back tears.

"Hey," he whispered. "We're together now. That's what matters."

"But I wasted time I could have spent with you. That we could have spent with each other."

"It might have felt like years to me, but it was only a few weeks in the scheme of things, Veronica." He drew back a little and looked down at her. "Besides, I knew it was only a matter of time before I had you exactly where you are right now."

"At the wedding?"

"No, in my arms."

CHAPTER SEVENTEEN

THEY SETTLED into a routine almost immediately. Jasper stayed with her for three nights after the wedding. When he asked her if she was ready to come stay with him, she said she was.

And, once she saw his house, she understood why he wanted her to come to him. Her apartment was nice. Cozy, clean, and calm

Jasper's home though? It was spacious and it had anything and everything her dream home would have.

Though he had a formal living room, they spent most of their time in what he called the *den*. In reality, it was basically a mancave. Slouchy furniture in a fantastic greige was spaced throughout the room. A huge flatscreen television was mounted to the wall. It was also hooked up to some sort of lighting system that emanated from behind the TV. The colors of the lights mimicked the screen, giving anyone in the room the sensation that they were immersed. The couches even had surround sound speakers *inside* the arms and back.

He also had every streaming service known to man, explaining that, with his work schedule, by the time he got home, all he wanted to do was unwind. He didn't get to watch often, but he liked to do that with a television series or movie. Sometimes he watched soccer or hockey. Occasionally even a boxing match or a MMA fight.

Veronica understood. She felt the same way about reading romance novels. That was how she liked to unwind.

What she liked even more is that he was perfectly content for her to curl up against his side and read while he watched television.

He didn't cook often, again because of his work schedule, but when he did, it was delicious. Jasper appreciated when she cooked for them as well.

After the first week, they talked and agreed that they weren't ready to spend time apart unless they had to, so they came up with a schedule. From Sunday to Tuesday, Jasper would stay at her apartment. From Wednesday to Saturday, she would stay with him at his house. They also agreed that they would talk to each other if they didn't feel like it was working out well.

Fortunately, their first week of that schedule seemed to work out well for both of them. Even though they'd only been dating for two weeks and five days, Veronica was more comfortable with Jasper than she'd ever been with anyone else. Even her own parents.

He truly accepted her for who she was. He wasn't a mind reader, but he paid attention. He asked how her day went, what her childhood was like, and who her best friend was.

When Veronica was embarrassed about her answers, he made her laugh by saying, "Hey, my answers to those questions are even more boring. I worked at my computer all day, my childhood was a montage of pranks, fights with my brother and cousins, and getting grounded. Which is what makes my last answer the craziest—my brother is my best friend. Apparently, trying to kill each other in our formative years solidified our relationship."

"I think you're the closest thing to a best friend I've had in a long time. Maybe even my entire life," she admitted.

That had effectively ended the discussion because Jasper stared at her with burning black eyes for a long moment before he got to his feet. He came over to her, hoisted her off the stool she was perched on (they were in the kitchen), and carried her back to his bedroom with her head dangling down his back.

Afterwards, Veronica lay face down on his bed, her head turned toward him, and Jasper rolled onto his side to look at her. He traced his fingertips down her spine, just touching her. It was something he often did. Random touches when they were making dinner together or hanging out. Hugs and kisses when she least expected them.

She hadn't brought it up, but she had no doubt that he sensed how desperately she needed that contact. He paid attention to her needs and reactions, even if she hadn't voiced them aloud yet. Not only did he pay attention, but he made an effort to give her what she needed. It was another reason she was done falling in love with him. She was already there.

"I'm going to have to call you my best friend more often," she murmured.

He smiled at her words, but his expression quickly turned serious. "As much as I like hearing that, you need friends and other people in your life, baby. The selfish part of me doesn't want you to do it because I like being your only touchstone, but the part of me that understands humanity knows that wouldn't be healthy for either one of us."

God, he really was her best friend. He was more concerned with her mental health and happiness than what it might mean for him if she expanded her circle.

"I'm sure I don't have to tell you this," she murmured lazily. "But it's difficult for me to make friends."

"What about your boss?" he asked.

"What do you mean?"

"The way she talks to you is definitely much friendlier than employer/employee. I mean, I don't talk to my assistant like that. I respect her and she's been with me a long time, but we don't have that kind of relationship."

Veronica's eyes grew unfocused. "I do consider Dominique a friend, but we're not that close. She keeps everyone at a distance. Even me. So, she's not my best friend. I think she could be, but I can tell that's not what she wants."

"I wonder why," Jasper murmured.

"I'm not sure, but she's older than she appears. Most fae are. It wouldn't surprise me if she keeps humans at arm's length because she must watch us age and fade away."

"God, I hope not. That's grim."

"I know."

They lay in silence for a long time until Veronica finally broached a subject she'd been curious about since she first met Jasper.

"I have a personal question I want to ask you," she began. "But if it makes you uncomfortable to talk about, it won't hurt my feelings if you say so."

Jasper's eyes had been closed, but he slowly opened them as she spoke. "We're not discussing ex's, are we? Because I'm going to need plenty of alcohol when you tell me about yours."

She shook her head. "No, it's about your magic."

"Okay."

"I know magic is a very personal topic for most of us, and that a lot of supernaturals prefer not to share too much information, so if that's you—"

"Veronica, it's fine. Just asked me whatever it is you want to ask."

"Well, basically, I was wondering exactly what your magic *is*. There's a lot of mystery surrounding djinn and it's made me curious."

"Have you been dying to ask this since we met?" he teased, winking at her.

Veronica wrinkled her nose at him but told the truth. "Yes. Now, if you're willing, answer me."

"I'm sure you've heard rumors about djinn magic, haven't you?"

She nodded.

"Well, some of them are true. Djinn can grant wishes, but we're not obligated by our magic like folklore says. We're encouraged by our power to fulfill it, but not forced. The stronger the djinn, the easier to resist the wish. Unless the wisher has their own strong magic. Then, it's much more difficult. It can still be done, but we have to battle our own magic and theirs, so it takes longer to wrestle the urge to grant the wish into submission. There's no cap on the wishes unless we want it to be so, but there is always a price to be paid. Anytime a djinn grants your wish, it sets the world, well, the magic in this world, out of balance. In order to maintain that balance, there has to be an equal payment. But it's not a basic trade, like two items of equal value. At least in a financial worth sense. The value is based on what you care about. If your wish is small, you pay with a small thing. Something that you value but may not miss too much. If the wish is big or mean-ingful, then you pay with the things you value most. Djinn get blamed for a lot of that, but it's not our choice. The magic itself is what required balance and so it's the magic that demands the price."

Veronica stared at him. "That's a heavy responsibility. Did you have your powers as a child?"

"To an extent. We don't fully mature into our power until the completion of puberty. I fully came into my power at seventeen."

"Wow, that's young."

"What about you?" he asked. "When did you fully come into your abilities?"

"I've always had them," she admitted. "Even as a kid."

Jasper fell silent. That was painful to hear. She'd never had a chance to be a child. She'd always carried the weight of other people's emotions on her shoulders. It was clear that Veronica loved her parents, but Jasper also got the sense that they didn't protect her as they should have.

"It is what it is," she murmured, her eyes closing as she sighed.

"I hate that saying," Jasper rasped, flattening his palm on the center of her back between her shoulder blades. He left it there, feeling her slow, deep breaths.

"Why?" she asked, her eyes still closed.

"It's too accurate. There are some things that just shouldn't happen, yet there's nothing to do be done about them. So, it's true that it is what it is, but it shouldn't be."

"You have a strong sense of justice," Veronica mumbled, her tone sleepy. "It's one of the reasons I love you."

Jasper didn't say anything else as she slid into sleep. But he didn't follow her. For a long time, he lay on his bed, feeling her back rise and fall beneath his hand, listening to her quiet breathing, and he wished he could have protected her twenty years ago when she was just a little girl.

CHAPTER EIGHTEEN

THEY HIT their first major bump in the road a week later. Veronica should have known that it was too easy.

She didn't get out of the office until late on Friday night. Dominique had finally put out an ad for an administrative assistant. Once they'd hired and trained someone, quite a bit of Veronica's time would be freed up because she wouldn't be handling basic paperwork and bookkeeping tasks.

Until then, she and Dominique were both working ten- and twelve-hour days just trying to keep up with everything.

It was her night to go to Jasper's. The rotation suited her for now, but it was early days still. Veronica wasn't sure how she would feel in a month or two. Right now, she was just enjoying her time with him.

When she pulled into his driveway, there was a strange car parked in front of the house. For a second, Veronica thought about going to the front door and ringing the bell. If he had company, she hated the idea of waltzing right into his house.

Then again, if he was dealing with business, she didn't want to interrupt that by ringing the doorbell.

After vacillating for a few moments, Veronica finally drove around to the garage. She used the opener that Jasper had given her and opened the garage door. Her car slotted in neatly between Jasper's Range Rover and a low-slung black sports car that he occasionally drove. Once the car was off, she took a slow breath. The day had been stressful and now she wasn't sure what she was walking into. Surely, if it was something important, Jasper would have texted her. A quick check of her phone revealed that he hadn't. Maybe it was just a friend, then.

She gathered her purse and her laptop bag and walked over to the door leading into the mudroom. Once the garage door was down, she opened the door to the mudroom and kicked off her shoes. Her purse was hung on a hook, and she stooped down to pick up her heels. As comfortable as they were, no shoes felt good after twelve hours wearing them.

Her footsteps were almost silent as she padded through the mudroom and laundry room and into the kitchen. As soon as she stepped inside, she froze.

Jasper stood across the kitchen, his back against the countertop of the coffee station, and a woman with long, dark hair was practically climbing him as though she wanted to devour him.

At first, the sight was like a punch to the gut. A sound escaped her, half groan and half sob. Jasper and the woman broke apart, turning toward her. With her brain still stuck on what she'd just seen, Veronica felt nothing from either of them. Only her own pain.

Especially when she saw the woman's face. It was Jasmine Shah, Prema's younger sister. And she wore a smug smile.

It was that smile that broke through the haze of pain and disappointment that clouded her mind. Veronica suddenly focused on the woman and sensed her triumph and her loathing. That, coupled with the satisfied smirk on the woman's face, told Veronica all she needed to know about what she walked in on.

Jasper's mental shields were completely down. His emotions careened wildly from anger to sadness, to absolutely fury. None of it was directed at her. No, it was all for Jasmine.

"Veronica—"

She lifted her hand, stopping his words. Jasper fell silent. Veronica tried to give him a reassuring look, but he didn't seem to notice. So, she focused on Jasmine, whose smug smile was now a wide, wicked grin. Though she was no telepath, Veronica could still almost hear the other woman's thoughts. She'd planned this. She wanted to drive a wedge between Veronica and Jasper. Whether it was so she could truly have Jasper to herself or to "teach" Veronica some sort of lesson, it was unclear.

Either way, all she wanted to do was insert herself between the couple and drive them apart.

Well, that wouldn't be happening.

Putting her hands on her hips, Veronica stared the other woman down. She hated confrontation, but it was clear that Jasmine's machinations weren't going to end until it happened. If that was what the younger woman wanted, that was what she would get.

"You need to grow up," Veronica said.

"Excuse me?" Jasmine said, the picture of affront.

"Your jealousy and bitterness aren't hurting anyone but you."

"That wasn't what you were saying when you walked into the kitchen and saw Jasper kissing me."

Before Veronica could reply, Jasper interrupted. "No. She walked in and saw you crawling all over me. The only time I touched you was to push you away, but you came right back at me before I could even tell you no."

The temperature in the room ratcheted up a few notches and Jasmine's confident demeanor took a hit.

"You should tell her the truth, Jasper," she said, trying to salvage the drama she seemed intent on having. "You should tell her that you've been seeing me behind her back every chance you get."

This time it was Veronica who scoffed. Jasmine glared at her, her eyes narrow and her fists clenched. "Denial isn't a good look, halfling."

Jasper's body went rigid at the slur that Jasmine threw at Veronica, but she didn't give him a chance to intervene.

"It would be difficult for you two to be carrying on behind my back considering we've spent every night together since we returned from the wedding."

"You're not with him at his office," Jasmine shot back, once again smug.

"No, but his mother is, and she's been calling and texting me off and on all week. I doubt very much she would be doing that if you were holing up in Jasper's office with him for a nooner."

Jasmine blinked at her, but Veronica saw Jasper's lip twitch.

"You also don't realize that I'm an empath, Jasmine. I can feel everything you're feeling. Mostly because you don't even bother trying to shield yourself. Your thoughts are so loud that I can hear some of them. I know you're lying. It's leaking off you with every breath you take." Veronica paused to take a calming breath. "And I can feel Jasper's emotions. He wasn't happy with you at the wedding, but now? He's repulsed by you. I can feel it. Even if you succeeded in separating us, he would still loathe you for what you've done today."

Jasmine whirled toward Jasper. "Is that true?" she asked.

"It is. What you did today is cruel and cold. Even if I didn't have Veronica any longer, I wouldn't want anything to do with you."

Those words finally seemed to pierce the thick hide of denial that Jasmine had wrapped around herself.

"What a horrible thing to say," she whispered.

Jasper released a harsh bark of laughter. "A horrible thing to say? You came into my home and forced yourself on me because you're jealous and spoiled. You want your way no matter the cost or the pain it causes anyone else. Yet I'm the horrible one?"

Jasmine's face paled and then hardened. Veronica knew before the woman spoke that she was going to make it even worse.

"I wish you would break things off with her and never see her again," Jasmine said.

Veronica couldn't believe that she had the gall to try and use Jasper's magic against him, knowing it would push him to grant her wish.

An evil gleam entered Jasmine's eyes as magic swelled around them. The kitchen heated up even more, as though the room itself were in a large oven. Veronica watched in awe as Jasper seemed to grow in height and breadth, his skin taking on a darker red hue and his black hair and eyes shifting and shimmering with the ghostly trace of fire.

"You dare?" he asked, his voice deep and resonant, filled to the brim with magic and anger. "You dare try to use my own magic against me?"

Veronica knew from their conversation a couple of weeks ago that Jasper's magic would encourage him to fulfill the wish, but that he would ultimately get to choose whether he did. She assumed Jasmine was a powerful djinn based on the tension running through Jasper's body. The scent of wood smoke entered the kitchen, and a small flame raced along the edge of the countertop behind Jasper.

After a few tense moments, he released a long breath, and his body seemed to relax. His skin returned to the normal olive tone, and his body no longer seemed as large. The fire behind him snuffed out with a puff of smoke, leaving a small scorch mark on the countertop.

"You are no longer welcome in my home, Jasmine. Ever. And I will be speaking to my mother about what you tried to do here today so she understands when I refuse to ever be in your presence again. If I see you on the street, you will be a stranger to me. If you call me or speak to me, I won't hear your voice. You no longer exist in my world."

"I'm your sister-in-law!" she cried, gesturing wildly. "You're going to have to see me sometimes."

"Maybe. Maybe not. I don't have to do anything I don't want to do, and I no longer want to deal with you." He went in for the kill after that. "And my mother will not be happy when she hears about what happened here tonight."

"Your mother is the one who picked me for you!" she hissed.

"No, she thought we could attend the wedding together. She wasn't choosing you as my bride." With those words, his eyes moved to Veronica, making it clear who he was choosing.

Jasmine tossed her hair. "I expect an apology the next time I see you," she said to Jasper. She pretended Veronica wasn't even in the room. Apparently, that was her answer to the situation—more denial.

"The next time you see me, I won't see you."

With a huff, Jasmine turned and stomped out of the kitchen. Her angry footsteps clacked against the hardwood floor. Neither Jasper nor Veronica followed her. A few moments later, the front door opened and then slammed shut, the crack echoing throughout the house.

"Well, that was fun," Jasper said, leaning back against the counter and crossing his arms over his chest. His tone was wary when he asked, "Are you okay?"

"Yes, I'm fine," Veronica answered, wondering why he was maintaining distance between them.

He pushed off the counter and came toward her. "Are you sure?"

"Yes. I don't like confrontations, but it was clear that was necessary."

"You understand she was lying through her teeth about us seeing each other behind your back, right?"

Veronica nodded. "I knew. Even before she spoke."

"It still hurt you to see her all over me like that, though."

She nodded again, hugging her waist. "More than I thought it would. More than it probably should since we've been dating less than a month."

"Don't talk like that," Jasper insisted, coming even closer. "We both know what this is and where it's going. That's all that matters."

"Do you think she'll make things difficult between you and your mother?"

Jasper shook his head. "No. Maybe between Milo and Prema and I, but I doubt it'll last long. They both know what she's like."

"What's that?"

"Spoiled rotten and unable to understand the word no."

Veronica nodded. That seemed accurate.

"My mother really likes you, you know. Even if Jasmine went running to her, telling tales, Leila would be on your side."

"I don't know, Jasper. She did try to arrange for you to take Jasmine to the wedding as your date."

He came even closer, stopping just in front of her. Jasper leaned forward, resting his hands on the counter on each side of her body. "Only because she knew I'd come alone otherwise, and she didn't want to deal with all the questions and gossip flying around the wedding. The day was about Milo and Prema, as it should have been. My single status would have been a distraction."

"Are you sure she doesn't care that I'm an empath?" Veronica asked.

He shook his head. "I told her Thursday after we arrived that you were an empath, and I didn't want her scaring you off. That was all it took, really. She might be tough and a meddler, but she wants me to be happy, first and foremost. You make me happy, which means she automatically approves of you. Oh, and you didn't fall at my feet immediately when I asked you out, which makes her like you even more. She said I would appreciate you the way you deserved if I had to work for you."

Veronica had no response to that.

Jasper continued, "I just hope you won't make me work too hard to get you to marry me. Even though I screwed up and told my parents about your abilities before you had a chance."

She gaped at him. She heard his admission that he messed up, but her brain was still stuck on his first statement. It took a few seconds before she managed to squeak, "Marry you?"

"I've already explained to Leila that we won't be having a three-ring circus for a wedding. That it will be very small, just immediate family, because you shouldn't have to endure the same kind of huge event that Milo and Prema had. She didn't argue. Probably because I mentioned that I wanted to try and talk you into starting our family in the next year or two. The woman is rabid for grandchildren."

Veronica blinked at him, her mouth opening and closing, but no sound emerging.

Finally, Jasper asked, "Any thoughts on the matter or are you going to stare at me all night?"

"I-I-I'm not sure what to say," she stammered. Her brain seemed to be stuck on the words "married" and "starting a family."

"Say you'll marry me," Jasper supplied.

"Now?" Her voice cracked as she asked the question.

He laughed. "Maybe not now. In a few months."

"A few months?" she repeated, still blinking over and over.

He laughed again, wrapping his arms around her waist. "I'll give you as much time as you need, but you should know that I'm going to try and change your mind every chance I get."

Finally, Veronica regained control of her brain and mouth. She sighed. The man was always throwing her off balance. "Ask me again in a couple of months."

He kissed her lightly. "I will." Another kiss. "But I still want you to move in with me before then."

Oh, that wasn't fair. She wanted so badly to say yes, but it was too much, too soon.

"I'll ask you again next week." When she opened her mouth, he continued talking, "And the next week. And the week after that. And however many weeks it takes until you're comfortable with the idea." He paused. "To be clear, I can accept a no. I just want you to understand that this is what I want. I don't ever want you to feel like you have to guess anything with me. So, when I ask you every week, it's not to pressure you. It's so you know you're welcome…when you're ready."

"I understand."

He smiled. "Good. Now, I'm starving. We should order in tonight. I don't feel like cooking."

Just like that, the awkward conversations were over. No sulking, no pouting, no negative emotions pouring off him. Jasper rolled with the punches, got up and kept right on going. He wasn't stewing or brooding. Just…living his life.

"Sounds good," Veronica said. "I want pizza."

"Then, I guess we're having pizza."

"Are you always going to give me my way?" she asked.

He shrugged. "Probably. Is that going to be an issue?"

Veronica shook her head. He could spoil her whenever he wanted.

EPILOGUE

One month later

Veronica was at her wit's end. Every applicant they got for the administrative assistant position was a poor fit. They were nice enough people, but they either didn't have the experience or the patience for the type of work that would be required of them.

Sighing heavily, she tried to focus on the spreadsheet on her screen. She couldn't work late today because, as of tonight, she was moving in with Jasper. They planned to spend the weekend getting all her things brought over. Anything she didn't want to keep was being sold or donated.

She had to get the work done before five because she would not be late for her first night of officially living with Jasper. And, just as he predicted, his parents had taken his side in regard to Jasmine. They were awesome.

Her own parents were ecstatic for her. Her mom was so excited that she finally met a man who loved her exactly how she was. Veronica was pretty sure her parents liked Jasper even more than they liked her. Well, maybe not, but sometimes it seemed so.

Also, as Jasper predicted, his brother and Prema had handled the issue of Jasmine well. Prema apologized for her sister's behavior, though Veronica told her it wasn't necessary, and explained that Jasmine had developed a pretty intense crush on Jasper as soon as the families had all met. She thought the wedding would be her chance to have him see her for who she really was.

According to Prema, Jasmine was embarrassed by her behavior and had started dating a very nice man that Milo met through work.

As she contemplated all of the this, the front door to the office opened and an older woman strutted in, her short auburn hair styled in a sleek bob. Pale skin glowed with vitality and there was nary a wrinkle in sight, but something about the way she held herself gave Veronica the impression that she was older than she appeared.

That and all her emotions were buried beneath a vault made of stone. There was no stray threat of anger or happiness hanging from her anywhere.

She walked right up to Veronica's desk and held out her hand. Without thinking, Veronica put her hand in the woman's and shook it.

"Hello, dear. My name is Zelda Forest and I'm here about the administrative assistant position."

Veronica smiled, but she knew it didn't reach her eyes. She was afraid to hope this woman would be the answer to their staffing issues. "Lovely. Well, why don't we start off by having you fill out an application. Once that's done, I'll chat with my boss and see if we can do a quick interview this afternoon. Does that sound okay?"

The woman nodded. "It sounds great to me."

She reached into her desk and pulled out one of the tablets they used to intake new clients. Veronica pulled up the employment application. This was a bit of a test. Supernaturals were often older than they appeared. Many older ones didn't like technology, but it was necessary in our business because there was no way they could handle the workload without it.

She stood and realized the woman was much taller than she originally thought. Even though Veronica wore three-inch heels, she towered over her. She was even taller than Dominique.

"If you'll follow me, we'll get you set up in the conference room so you can fill out the application."

Veronica led her into the room and handed her the tablet. "Take as much time as you need. If you have a resume to submit, I'll give you my email address before you leave and you can send it to me online."

Zelda smiled at her, her expression serene. "Of course, dear. Thank you for letting me do this without an appointment."

"If you're a good fit, I'm going to be thanking you. Profusely."

Her smile widened and her eyes sparkled with humor and…magic. Veronica didn't ask because it was the height of rudeness, but she did wonder what sort of supernatural Zelda was.

She left the conference room, shutting the door behind her, and went back to her desk. Veronica glanced at the older woman once and saw that she was navigating the tablet with no apparent issues, taking the stylus from the holder on the side and moving quickly through the screens.

Feeling hopeful, she turned back to her computer just as the front door opened again. Veronica froze completely when she looked up and saw the man entering.

He was beautiful. That was the only way to describe him. His hair was dark brown, almost black, and his eyes were a piercing blue. His face belonged in magazines and on television because the women of the world deserved to see it.

He prowled into the office with the air of a predator. He wore a glamour, but it was such a good one that she almost missed it. She could feel his "otherness" from his emotions though. Not that Veronica could get a clear read on him. He was fae, that much was clear, and her empathic abilities often didn't work on them due to her fae ancestry. Their magic interfered with her sense of them.

Honestly, if Veronica wasn't so utterly in love with Jasper, she would have been tempted by this man. As it was, she was nearly speechless due to his gorgeousness.

Finally, she snapped out of it. "Good afternoon. How can I help you?" she asked, rising and coming out from behind her desk.

The man stopped a few feet away. "I'm here to see Dominique Proxa."

Holy cow, his voice was just as good as the rest of him—raspy, deep, and with a hint of a drawl. He sounded like Sam Elliott's younger, gruffer brother.

Veronica managed to speak again without stuttering. "Do you have an appointment?"

"No, but she'll want to see me."

"Your name?"

"Ronan Byrne."

Her scalp tingled at the name. It sounded familiar...then, it hit her. The Byrnes were one of the ruling families in the magic realm.

"Let me see if she's available. We may have to schedule an appointment for you later today or this week."

His expression told her that he doubted he'd have to wait. That arrogance pierced through the spell his appearance had cast on her and Veronica barely suppressed the urge to roll her eyes at him. He must have sensed it because he smirked, as though she amused him.

Veronica went to Dominique's door and knocked. After a moment, her boss called out, "Come in, Veronica." She sounded distracted.

Normally, she would have just stuck her head in the door and told Dominique there was someone who wanted to see her, but she didn't want Ronan overhearing any of their conversation. Veronica walked inside, shutting the door behind her, and came to sit in the chair across from Dominique.

"Give me just a sec," her boss said, her fingers moving rapidly over her computer keyboard. After a few minutes, she turned toward Veronica. "What's up?"

"There's a man here to see you and..." Veronica trailed off. She wasn't sure how to word her thoughts.

"Is he giving you trouble?" Dominique asked, her expression shutting down and growing cold.

"Not exactly. But he seems to think you'll want to talk to him."

"What's his name?"

"Ronan Byrne."

"As in the Byrnes in Magic?" Magic was the informal name for the realm of supernaturals.

"I think so. I don't recognize the name but he's definitely arrogant enough to be a member of the fae court."

"All right. Show him in, but if I buzz you once, come in and tell me that I have to leave if I'm going to make my next appointment in time."

"I can do that."

Veronica walked out of her boss's office. She shot a look over to the conference room, but Zelda was no longer sitting there.

"The woman left a note and a tablet on your desk," Ronan said. "She said she would be in touch soon."

A bit disappointed and confused, Veronica focused on him. "Dominique will see you now."

His smug smile said that he knew that would be the case. Veronica wondered if he assumed they knew who he was. And wondered how much of a loop it would throw him for if she asked if he was a member of the ruling Byrne family.

She wouldn't do it, of course, because that wasn't her way, but that didn't mean she wasn't tempted.

Ronan followed her into Dominique's office. As soon as he entered, her boss stood up and walked around her desk, smoothing the long skirt she wore over her hips. They both froze, stock still, staring at each other.

Simultaneously, they said, "It's you."

Veronica looked between them, confused. Did they know each other?

Dominique glanced at her, her expression calm and aloof as ever, but Veronica could sense how flustered she was. "Could you excuse us, Veronica?"

Curious, Veronica nodded and left the office, shutting the door behind her. With the soundproofing Dominique had invested in for the office, she wouldn't be able to hear anything being said. Her inquisitiveness would have to remain unsatisfied unless her boss decided to tell her what happened.

Frustrated, Veronica went to her desk and picked up the sticky note Zelda had placed on top of the tablet.

Veronica,

   I completed the application and I am very interested in a position. Unfortunately, I received an urgent call so I had to leave. I took the liberty of taking one of your business cards. Your email address is listed there, so I'll forward you my resume later today.
   Z

Zelda had signed the note with a large, ornate Z and written her phone number beneath it. Grateful that the woman hadn't left because she decided she didn't want the job, Veronica sat back down at her desk and began the process of downloading the woman's application from the cloud.

Half her mind was still in Dominique's office, wondering how her boss knew Ronan. And at her obvious reaction to him. Dominique very rarely got ruffled. And she never, ever lost her temper or raised her voice. She wasn't laid back. Her demeanor was proper and almost cold with people she didn't know well. With Veronica, she'd warmed up quite a bit, but there was still distance between them. Distance initiated by Dominique.

Veronica's phone vibrated on her desk, and she glanced at the screen. It was Jasper.

> Jasper: What time should I be at your apartment with the truck?

He'd insisted on hiring a small U-haul truck to carry her things to storage. She'd already brought several boxes of things she intended to keep to his home, but they were going to get the rest of it tonight.

Just like that, her mind was off her boss and the mysterious man in her office and on the man she loved.

> Veronica: I'm leaving at four. Can you be there by five?

> Jasper: Not before?

> Veronica: I still have a few things to pack.

> Jasper: I can help. The quicker you get done, the quicker I can take you home.

A thrill shot through her. Home. What was his house was now going to be her home, too.

> Veronica: I'll be at my apartment by four-thirty. See you then.

> Jasper: Love you 🤍

> Veronica: Love you too. 😚

Veronica decided she'd tell Jasper about Ronan tonight and the strange interaction her boss had with him. Though he wasn't empathic as she was, he was observant and insightful. Maybe he would be able to glean something from the situation that she hadn't been able to.

Smiling to herself, Veronica got back to work. She wanted to get everything done and go home to the man she loved.

Want to know who sabotaged the pull-out couch during Milo's wedding weekend? Read the exclusive bonus scene here!

There's also another extended bonus scene featuring Jasper and Veronica and...wedding bells?

ACKNOWLEDGMENTS

I haven't done one of these lately because I'm always worried I'll leave someone out.

Still, I feel like I need to thank a bunch of people who have helped me with my last few books, including this one. They are a huge part of the reason I'm still writing and publishing. So, I'm going to give this a try and not beat myself up too badly if I forget someone.

To Jena, you always manage to create covers for me that fit my vision, even when I struggle to describe what I'm looking for (or find the right image). I always appreciate your patience with my tendency to forget…everything.

Nikki, you're not only my best friend, you are one of the best editors a girl could have. I love seeing your thoughts on my stories, even if you don't like something. Your comments always make me laugh.

Ellie Rae, you caught things that 4 beta readers, an editor, and this author missed. Thanks for putting your eyeballs on this story and making it better.

To the Best Betas! Chantell, Courtney, Michele, and Nicole, y'all are such a huge help with each and every book. You catch my plot holes and are excellent brainstorming partners when I'm stuck or I'm trying to outline the next book. I couldn't do this without your feedback and your encouragement. Because, let's face it, I probably would have given up writing and gone to live in a cave if I didn't get the occasional pep talk from y'all.

Also, I have to thank my Feral Females—Elana, Jennifer, and Tabby. Our group chat gives me so much inspiration, especially the memes and our banter! Keep being awesome! (And I promise none of your names will be used when I'm writing things in my future books. Your secrets will be safe-ish with me!)

To the Husbot and Lil Bit—thank you for your patience when I'm deep in the writing cave and you have to fend for yourselves. I know it gets tedious when I keep asking for "Five more minutes" when we're supposed to go somewhere or do family game night but you never get upset or angry. Also, Husbot, thank you for contributing at least one character trait to every male main character in my books and being my real life book boyfriend.

Finally, last but certainly not least, to my readers. Thank you for reading my stories and sticking with me when things got hard in my personal life and I wasn't able to publish as often. If at least one of you laughed or grinned while you read this book, I feel like I did my job well. I'm glad you find the characters and stories that live in my head as entertaining as I do. I love getting to share them with you and not worry that you think I'm nuts. I mean, we know that I'm nuts, but I'm assuming you like that if you've read more than one or two of my books.

ABOUT THE AUTHOR

Born and raised in Texas, C.C. Wood writes saucy paranormal and contemporary romances featuring strong, sassy women and the men that love them. If you ever meet C.C. in person, keep in mind that most of her characters are inspired by people she knows, so anything you say or do is likely to end up in a book one day.

A self-professed hermit, C.C. loves to stay home, where she reads, writes, cooks, and watches TV. She can usually be found drinking coffee or a cocktail as she spends time with her hubby and daughter.

ALSO BY C.C. WOOD

NSFW Series:

In Love With Lucy

Earning Yancy

Tempting Tanya

Chasing Chelsea

Paranormal Romance:

Bitten Series:

Bite Me

Once Bitten, Twice Shy

Bewitched, Bothered, and Bitten

One Little Bite

Love Bites

Bite the Bullet

Blood & Bone Series (Bitten spin-off)

Blood & Bone

Souls Unchained

Forevermore (Contains Destined by Blood)

Ensnared in Shadow

-

Paranormal Romcom:

Mystical Matchmakers:

Rock and Troll

Lady and the Vamp

Suddenly My Selkie

Djinn in Love

Fae-King It (coming Spring 2025)

Devil Springs: Available in Kindle Unlimited!

Kidnapped by the Vampire

Chased by the Alpha

Hidden by the Gargoyle

Taken by the Blood God

<u>**Paranormal Cozy Romcom:**</u>

The Wraith Files: Available in Kindle Unlimited!

Don't Wake the Dead

The Dead Come Calling

Raise the Dead

Made in United States
North Haven, CT
29 June 2025

70210641R00104